streets

of

death

Our Playwright may show
In some fifth act what this wild drama means.

The Play, ALFRED, LORD TENNYSON

streets
of
death

ONE

MENDOZA CAME INTO THE KITCHEN, hat in hand, and asked, "Feeling better, *cara*?" Mrs. MacTaggart was just starting on the breakfast dishes. Alison was hunched over a cup of coffee at the kitchen table, her red hair slightly tousled, still in her robe. She gave him a glance of burning resentment.

"Ah, she'll be fine," said Mrs. MacTaggart.

"If I had ever," said Alison, "dreamed—hic—after I felt so fine all the time I was carrying the twins, that—hic—this time I'd develop morning sickness, I'd never have—damn—" She leaped up and fled precipitately for the bathroom at the end of the hall.

"Poor lamb," said Mrs. MacTaggart. "But she's near three months along now, it should clear away in a bit."

"I certainly hope so," said Mendoza. "I'm beginning to feel like an outcast around here, Mairí." Mrs. MacTaggart laughed as he went out the back door.

The four cats were sensibly indoors this chill January morning, but the twins, now officially four, were tearing around the backyard with Cedric the Old English sheepdog galumphing after them. They both hung on to his collar helpfully as Mendoza went out the gate, and then hung over the fence to watch him back out the Ferrari. He waved back at them, thanking God absently for Mairí MacTaggart; Terry and Johnny were a lively pair these days, none the worse for their accidental kidnapping last August, and in her present state Alison wasn't up to coping with them. He wasn't worried about Alison; the doctor said she'd be fine once she got past the morning sickness.

He hoped he wasn't beginning to feel his age, with a forty-sixth birthday coming up, but he felt a little stale and tired as he slid down the winding road toward Hollywood Boulevard, thinking of the various business on hand at the Robbery-Homicide office of LAPD headquarters. The perennial violence, death, blood and guilt which had to be looked at and reduced to reports and filed away. Always more of it coming along, seemingly faster and more furious than ever. Of all the cases on hand right now, still being looked at or eventually to be filed in Pending, only two really interested him, and there didn't seem to be much chance that either would be tidily cleared up soon. There was no handle at all on those queer rape-assaults, and as for the pretty boys—

Mendoza's mouth tightened, thinking of the pretty boys. Those three he'd like to catch up to, but there wasn't any handle there either.

For once he was early; it was five to eight when he walked into the office, and found Sergeant Lake talking to an agitated-looking citizen in the anteroom. In the communal sergeants' office Hackett, Landers and Palliser were in; Wednesday was Higgins' day off and the others would be drifting in. He went on into his office and found the report from the night watch centered on his desk. Lake followed him.

"Look, this guy was waiting when I got here," he said. "I don't think it's anything, but I suppose somebody's got to listen to him."

"About what?"

"He says, about a murder going to be committed. I think he's just got an imagination," said Lake.

"Shove him off on Art. You'd better check with the hospital and see if that Beaver woman can talk to us." Mendoza picked up the report in one hand and his new cigarette lighter with the other, and Lake took a step back, eyeing it nervously.

"Shove who off on me?" Hackett came in, looming bulkily as usual, and added, "If you don't set fire to the building with that flame-thrower you'll at least singe your mustache off some day. Where Alison found that thing—"

Mendoza regarded it rather fondly; he liked gadgets. It had been a Christmas present from Alison; it was an oversize revolver with a gleaming pearl handle and a fearsome-looking attachment on the barrel which emitted a flame like an acetylene torch when the trigger was pulled. He pulled it now, the flame belched, and he lit a cigarette. "Jimmy has a nut-case," he said. "But we have to listen to the citizens." Galeano and Conway came down the hall talking. Lake went back to the switchboard. Mendoza was glancing at the night report, and suddenly sat up and exclaimed, "*¡Mil rayos! ¡Es el colmo!*"

"What's up?"

"This damned—I'll bet you, here they are again!" said Mendoza angrily, slapping Shogart's report down on his desk. "Same M.O., same general area, and for God's sake—I'd better check with the hospital—Jimmy!"

Hackett scanned the report rapidly, and his eyes turned cold. "Our pretty boys all right, a hundred to one." Over the last two months, the trio had been described, well enough to mark them as the same, by seven senior citizens who had been attacked, mauled and robbed on the street. None of them had had much to be robbed of;

the biggest haul the thugs had got had been seven bucks. Two of the victims were still in the hospital. All the attacks had been in a radius of eight blocks, from Temple Street up to Beverly, and from the partial descriptions the men at Robbery-Homicide had pieced together a picture of the same three louts. All young, probably under twenty, one with long blond hair—"real handsome," said three of the victims—tall and thin, and dressed in natty sports clothes: two others, not as tall, one heavier than the other, also dressed in flashy clothes—an oddity for the area. And for whatever reason or lack of reason, they had used the wanton violence on the old people they had jumped: kicking, gouging, and clubbing. To date there had been four women, the youngest seventy, and three men, all over eighty: old people living little quiet lives in the inner city, on pensions, on Social Security, all but one of them living alone in tiny apartments, rented rooms.

And now this report, devoid of description, but Hackett would take a bet it was the eighth victim: found on the street by a Traffic unit at nine-twenty, just up from the Union Station behind the church at the Plaza, an elderly man in clerical clothes, no I.D., apparently beaten. He was in Central Receiving.

Mendoza was on the phone, looking grim. Sergeant Lake came in again and said plaintively, "Look, this guy is about to have kittens."

"All right, all right, I'll talk to him," said Hackett.

Mendoza put down the phone and stood up abruptly, yanking down his cuffs. As usual he was dapperly dressed, in dark-gray Dacron, snowy shirt, a discreet dark tie. He said, "Well, the hospital's found out who he is—he came to a while ago. It's Father O'Brien from the Mission Church."

"I will be damned," said Hackett.

"No, they will be," said Mendoza. "By the good God, Art, I'd like to get this unholy trio. I'm going over to see if he can give us anything."

"They wouldn't have got much from him either, I wouldn't think."

"They don't seem to care. You go talk to the nut. And somebody'll have to cover that Roundtree inquest." Mendoza took up his hat.

In the corridor, Henry Glasser was talking earnestly to their policewoman Wanda Larsen; Jason Grace had just come in. Palliser was on the phone in the other office, Galeano swearing as he typed a report, Conway and Landers arguing about something. The switchboard was keeping Lake busy. Another day was under way for the Robbery-Homicide office, and it looked as if it was to be the usual kind of day.

Hackett watched Mendoza out, and massaged his jaw, grinning a little to himself, humorlessly. Mendoza was as touchy as the devil about emotions, and nobody in the office made any cracks about his going back to church after many years as the professed agnostic; for some reason the pretty boys had got under Mendoza's skin anyway, but now that they'd jumped a priest he was really annoyed. It would be nice to get hold of some tangible lead to those boys, but Hackett didn't really hope for one.

He put the report on Mendoza's desk and went out to look at Jimmy's nut-case. As he came into the anteroom he ran into Lieutenant Carey, who had a manila envelope in one hand and was looking harassed.

"If you've got anything for us, go away. We've got enough to do already."

"I can't help it," said Carey. "It's a hundred percent sure this guy is dead. It's a homicide if not Murder One, so it's your business. I've got all these statements—"

"Tell it to Galeano or Landers," said Hackett resignedly.

"This is Sergeant Hackett, Mr. Yeager," Lake was saying. "You just tell your story to him."

"Yeah, yeah, I got to tell somebody, you got to do something about it, I been up half the night worrying and I said to myself, I got to tell the cops, we got to do something, see, and so I came—"

"Just come in here and sit down, Mr. Yeager," said Hackett soothingly. Yeager might be a nut at that. He was a scrawny middle-aged man in a shabby brown suit; he had a prominent Adam's apple that bobbed up and down as he talked, and bulging pale-blue eyes, and a high reedy voice. Hackett settled him in the chair beside his desk and prepared to listen. There were other things he could be doing. That Beaver woman who'd been assaulted and raped ought to be able to answer questions sometime today; there was that inquest—a straightforward suicide; there'd been other things on the night-watch report, by the length of it, and without much doubt something new would show up today. But cops got paid by taxpayers, and had to listen to them when they came in. "What's it all about, Mr. Yeager?" he asked.

"Well, it's about a murder," said Yeager nervously. "I didn't hardly know what to do, but my God, I got to do something—I been worried to death—I didn't hardly believe it but I— Listen, I don't like the guy, he's given me a hard time, and his ma too, always complainin' about the furnace makin' noise and the faucets drip and like that, but my God, I never thought he'd do a thing like that! A murder!"

"Now slow down and let's have it from the beginning," said Hackett patiently. "What murder?"

"His own ma, for God's sake! They live together, see,

and I'm the manager of the apartment. This lady, Mis' Lampert, she's a widow, no other kids, and he's a young guy but he don't work, she does. At a dress shop someplace. And he's got a girl friend comes to see him afternoons, and I heard 'em talk about killing the old lady to get her money." Yeager paused, breathing hard.

"Heard them? How? Where were they?"

"Uh—in the apartment," said Yeager uneasily. "Uh—the door was kind of open and I was fixing the window in the hall."

Hackett sat back and his chair creaked. "Well, now, people do some funny things, Mr. Yeager, but it's a little hard to believe this pair would go discussing a murder with the door open and other people around. Are you sure you didn't just misunderstand something they said?"

"No, I didn't! They was talking about killing her!" said Yeager excitedly. "Listen, you got to do something about it—"

Hackett sighed. Across the room he saw Carey gesticulating at Galeano and Conway, and Palliser was still on the phone. Landers was on the way out, and Jason Grace typing a report. "Now, Mr. Yeager—"

Mendoza bent over the hospital bed. "He's only been conscious the once," said the nurse. "It's a bad concussion, they'd have operated already except for his heart. When we got in touch with his own doctor—"

"Can you hear me, Father? Can you try to tell us who did this?" Three mornings ago, Mendoza had listened to the old priest say Mass at the little church in the old Plaza: a very traditional Mass, nothing new and progressive about Father Joseph Patrick O'Brien. He was probably in his eighties: a stocky, round little man with a broad snub-nosed Irish face, scanty hair and eyebrows. He lay on his back, his breathing slow and irregular, and Mendoza straightened up.

"The doctors don't think there's a good chance," said the nurse in a troubled tone. She was slim and black and rather pretty. "It's just terrible what goes on, a priest, and such an old man—just terrible."

Unexpectedly the man in the bed opened his eyes and stared up at them, moving his head slightly. A frown of pain creased his forehead and the nurse moved instinctively to quiet him.

"Can you hear me, Father? Can you tell me anything about who attacked you?"

The faded blue eyes fixed on Mendoza's face. "I— know you," the old priest whispered faintly. "Of course. I was—just about—get in the car. Who—who? Young— thugs. Three, I think—the one blond—and a loud plaid jacket—"

Mendoza sighed. "All right, that's enough for now, Father."

One veined hand crept up to his chest, and the priest went on, "My crucifix. All they got—no money—it was dark—but there were three of them. Tore my crucifix off—" His eyes shut again and he relaxed limply.

"Poor old man," said the nurse.

That was about all they'd get, thought Mendoza, but so far as it went it showed the pattern. Only what had O'Brien been doing down there at that time of night? Not that it mattered. There was a little pattern to this. The other seven all lived in the general area; most of them had been on their way home, at reasonably early hours—seven, eight, the latest attack had been at nine-thirty. By the little they got from the victims, it looked like the random thing —the pretty boys were jumping any senior citizen they

came across when the urge hit them: the old, lame, frail
senior citizens who wouldn't fight back.

The rest of them had been in that area unavoidably,
as residents; how had the priest happened to be there?
Mendoza was aware that the priests who served the little
church, nearly the oldest building in the city, no longer had
quarters there. In any case, somebody ought to be told
about O'Brien.

He drove down to the old Plaza, found the church
open, and went in. The little place was dim as a cavern,
only the flickering light at the altar moving, and the statues
along the walls seemed to loom taller than usual. A man
was speaking somewhere; following the voice, Mendoza
came to a tiny robing room past the confessional box, and
unexpectedly into a very small square room furnished as
an office, with desk and swivel chair. A tall thin young
man in clerical dress was talking on the phone, looked at
Mendoza in surprise, and at the offered badge with con-
sternation.

"I'm afraid I have some bad news for you." Mendoza
had seen him once or twice, the assistant priest here.

"About Father O'Brien—we knew something had happened, I was just calling the police again. When he didn't
come home last night—" He listened to what Mendoza
had to tell him, obviously distressed, and said, "I must go
to him. If he's as bad as you say—" But he answered questions as they went up to the church door. He and O'Brien
both had living quarters in the residence attached to the
much larger Church of the Blessed Sacrament in Hollywood. O'Brien sometimes stayed on down here, in his
little office, to write letters, as apparently he had last night.
He would have been driving one of the cars belonging to
the church, a ten-year-old Pontiac. The car, in fact, was

here—"I looked for it right away, we were afraid he'd had another heart attack when we realized he hadn't come home, and I came down at once—it's right where he always parked, behind the church."

"Yes, he said he was on his way to it," said Mendoza. No keys on him; the S.I.D. boys could have a look, but it was a long chance anything useful would show up. "Evidently he hadn't any money on him; the only thing they got was his crucifix."

The priest stopped and stared at him, one hand on the church door. "His crucifix—but that might give you some kind of clue, Lieutenant—that is, if it turned up in a pawnshop or somewhere. It's a very valuable antique— sterling silver set with a piece of Connemara marble. It was a gift from his old parish priest when he entered the seminary, and I believe it's several hundred years old. Any of us could identify it at once, if it should turn up anywhere."

Mendoza thanked him and watched him hurry up the street to a newish Ford. Let the S.I.D. boys come and go over the Pontiac for possible physical evidence, in case O'Brien had been jumped in or near it: a very small chance there'd be anything. Put out a description of the crucifix to the pawnshops, just in case.

He got into the big black Ferrari and lit a cigarette, thrusting the key into the ignition; his eyes were cold. Hackett was quite right: the pretty boys had got under Mendoza's skin. It was reasonless, in a way: it was only that much more of the sordid, wanton violence that stalked any big city in this year of grace, which any cop learned to live with. It wasn't a dramatic, important piece of crime, the kind that would get written up in the case-history books. The victims weren't good-looking or very interesting or important people. The louts, when they caught up to them—as by God they would, if the luck ran their way—probably would turn out to be two-bit thugs, not very interesting or important either, just thugs with low I.Q.'s.

But the pretty boys had touched Mendoza on the raw—Mendoza who had been looking at the blood and violence and death for nearly twenty-six years—because in a sense they were a stark symbol for all of it: all the incredibly brutal bloody happenstance of crime in the city.

He'd like to catch up to them. He tossed the cigarette out the window, laughed, and said to himself, *"¿Pues qué?"* Catch up to them, and then see one of the softheaded judges hand them a six-month sentence with time off for good behavior. He often wondered why he stayed on at this job.

Nick Galeano listened to what Carey had to say a little sleepily. He'd been on night watch for over two years, and his metabolism or something wasn't yet used to the different hours and sleeping at night. He was night-people anyway and wasn't operating on all cylinders until past noon. In a way he was glad of the change; there was usually more action on day watch, and more men to work with.

He'd only met Lieutenant Carey of Missing Persons a few times before. Carey was a serious, snub-nosed, stocky fellow who wore a perennially morose expression: possibly the result these days of all the myriad missing juveniles he had to look for, thought Galeano, yawning. But what he'd brought to Robbery-Homicide sounded more interesting and definitely offbeat.

"Look," he said, slapping his manila envelope down on Galeano's desk and shrugging massively at Galeano and Rich Conway. "I can't prove it's a homicide, but that's what it's got to add up to. It's a very funny one, boys. And

I've done all I can on it, and the man's got to be dead, so I bring it to you and let you go all round the mulberry bush on it. I mean, one way it's open and shut, but nobody'll ever prove anything—I don't think."

"Why not?" asked Conway, his gray eyes interested. "What's the case?"

"I'll give it to you short and sweet," said Carey. "Here's this Edwin Fleming. Twenty-nine, raised in Visalia, dropout from high school but no record. No relations—he was an only child; his father died when he was just a kid and his mother two years ago. He did a hitch in the Army and got sent to Germany, where he married this girl—her name is Marta, she's a reasonably good-looking blonde, twenty-six. This was four years ago. He gets out of the service, they come here, and he has trouble finding a job, finally gets one in construction—he'd done that before— only it's a small-time operation, kind of boss-and-one-helper thing, I gather. I'm just giving you the background. His wife has a baby about a year ago, and just after that he has an accident on the job—falls off a scaffold or something and ends up paralyzed. He was in and out of hospitals, but there wasn't anything the doctors could do—he was paralyzed from the waist down, and he'd never get better. The boss had insurance that paid for the hospitalization, but that was all—on account of technicalities here and there, Fleming wasn't eligible for any benefits from anybody, the government on down. So there he was, a useless hulk as you might put it, couldn't earn, had to be tended like a baby—oh, his mind was O.K., he could even get around some in a wheelchair, but he needed a good deal of attention."

"When does this tale get to be business for us?" asked Conway.

"Ten days ago," said Carey. "Eleven, now. A week

ago last Friday, when his wife reported him missing. A man in a wheelchair! It was damned fishy from the start, you can see that. They didn't have anything but what she could earn, she's working as a waitress at a restaurant on Wilshire, the Globe Grill. They had an old car, but they'd moved to this place on Westlake so she could walk to work, and they were trying to sell the car, she says she couldn't afford to run it. It's a six-family apartment and everybody else there is out at work all day except an old wino named Offerdahl who doesn't know anything and was probably too drunk to see anything there was to see. The Flemings lived on the second floor and he couldn't get the wheelchair downstairs by himself, obviously."

Galeano yawned again. "Where'd she leave the baby while she was at work?"

"Oh, they lost the baby about six months ago—it was a girl, I think, it got pneumonia or something and died. Anyway, she calls for cops—this was about six P.M. that Friday—and tells this tale, and of course it got passed on to me. I ask you!" said Carey, and sat back looking contemptuous. "She has the gall to tell me, all innocent and wide-eyed, that she comes home to find her husband gone— a man in a wheelchair—and the wheelchair's there, but he's missing. Vanished—whoosh—like that! He couldn't have crawled three feet by himself. She's afraid, she says, he's committed suicide, he'd been very despondent about his condition lately. I do ask you! If—"

"The wheelchair's still there?" repeated Galeano, suddenly fascinated. "That's like a magic trick." He had a brief ridiculous vision of angels snatching Fleming up to heaven, out of the wheelchair. Or little green men out of a UFO.

"The wheelchair's still there, and even if it wasn't, where could he go in it?" asked Carey reasonably. "Even if he'd managed to get downstairs with it, which he couldn't have? There isn't an elevator. Wheel himself over to Mac-Arthur Park and crawl into the lake?—even if he had thought of suicide, and there's not an iota of evidence he ever did. The people in that apartment didn't know them very well—they'd only been there a little over two months —but I've talked to people where they used to live, the few casual friends they have, and everybody says Fleming had adjusted pretty well to being a cripple, he'd talked about taking courses in handcrafts, maybe earning something that way."

"Have you dragged the lake in MacArthur?" asked Conway.

Carey uttered a rude word. "You can if you want. He'd have floated by now. I don't like having my intelligence insulted, is all. This dumb blonde bats her eyes at me and says he talked about suicide, he must've done it, she doesn't know how but he's gone, he must have killed himself. And a child of two could see there's no way! If he really wanted to commit suicide, he could have got out of a window—it's all cement sidewalk below—or cut his wrists or something, right there."

"Where was the blonde all day? Alibied? Anybody see him, and when and where?" asked Conway.

Carey snorted. "She was at work, like a good girl. Eight to two, and she was supposed to be back for the evening shift, seven to nine. Sure, a neighbor saw him—woman lives across the hall, a Mrs. Del Sardo, she left for work at the same time as the blonde and heard her say good-bye to Fleming, saw him in the wheelchair in the living room. If you ask me, the blonde timed it to have an alibi. And then she says, she had some shopping to do, she didn't come home till five o'clock and he was gone. Just gone."

"Leaving the wheelchair," said Galeano. The wheelchair had taken possession of his mind; the thing was like a conjuring trick.

"Look, it's kind of like one of those locked-room puzzles," said Carey, "and then again it's not. I mean, there's people all around—apartments, busy streets. Only nobody saw anything. And you remember it was raining like hell all that day. On the other hand, why would anybody see anything? That apartment house—everybody out at work except Fleming and old Offerdahl dead drunk down the hall."

"Yes, I see," said Conway. "Fleming almost completely helpless, on the second floor. And there's no smell of him anywhere?"

"Not a trace. And he'd be easy to trace, you can see. If you're feeling that energetic," said Carey, "you can have all the pipes examined, but I doubt that the blonde had time to murder and dismember him that thoroughly and feed him down the bathtub, say, before she called us. She's not a very big blonde, she wouldn't have had the strength to carry him anywhere, dead or alive—he was six feet, a hundred and eighty. You can see there's just one answer, it hits you in the eye."

"The boyfriend," said Galeano. "Yeah."

"I haven't turned one up, damn it. Good luck on it. All I see is that Fleming has got to be dead. I don't pretend to understand females," said Carey gloomily, "but however she may have felt about him once, here he was, a dead drag on her. He's no good to her as a husband, she's got to support him and take care of him, and he could live to be eighty. He didn't have any life insurance, he hadn't converted it when he got out of the service—that could explain why they didn't try to fake a suicide or accident. She d like to be rid of him, don't tell me she wouldn't. She—"

"And don't anybody say, she could walk out or divorce him," said Conway cynically. "The people we deal with aren't so logical. I suppose there's got to be a boyfriend."

"Go and look," said Carey. "They don't seem to have had many friends. They used to live over on Berendo in Hollywood, but I couldn't locate anybody who knew them. All I'll say is, the thing is obvious. There's got to be a boyfriend. She gave him a key, or he knocked on the door and Fleming let him in. He knocked him over the head—there's not a trace of blood in the place—and there's a driveway down the side to garages at back, he could've driven his car back there and lugged Fleming down to it in five minutes. Ten feet from the back door. Your guess is as good as mine what he might have done with him—maybe he's got a boat and dropped him out at sea, or buried him in his backyard—all I say is, Fleming's got to be dead, so it's your baby."

"The logic I follow," said Conway, "but what a bastard to work. But if there is a boyfriend, somebody's bound to know. The other girls she works with?"

"Four of 'em. They all say she's a loner, doesn't confide all girlish."

"What about her family?" asked Galeano.

"I said, she's German—married him over there. Oh, I guess she could have some family in Germany. I don't know."

"If she does, it could be she'd mentioned something in letters, but how to get at it—"

"No bets," said Carey. "I'll wish you good luck on it." He got up.

"Thanks so much," said Conway. "You know it'll end up in Pending—your files and ours."

"Well, I kind of hope you nail her," said Carey. "I

don't like having my common sense insulted. Vanished, she says, batting her eyes at me—this blonde. A man in a wheelchair, a cripple!"

"And the empty wheelchair there. I like that," said Galeano. "It's a nice touch somehow."

"Do have fun with it," said Carey.

Jason Grace and Tom Landers had been handed the new rape-assault because they'd been on the one last week, and the one last month, and this being in the same general neighborhood it might add up to the same X. The first two had been funny. "I hope," said Landers now, "we're not in for a spate of the offbeat ones. If this does match up."

"Oh, I don't know, relieves the monotony," said Grace. His chocolate-colored face with its dapper little mustache like Mendoza's was thoughtful as he reread the statement from the second victim. "Has Jimmy talked to the hospital yet?"

"I'll see."

The first victim, last month, had been a Mrs. Rena Walker over on Twentieth Street. Mrs. Walker was sixty-four, an upright and respectable widow, owned her own modest little house, and devoted much of her time to the Afro-American Methodist Church where she directed the choir. She said she'd just come home from grocery-shopping, about four that afternoon, when her doorbell rang and it was a boy asking about yard work. "I told him I couldn't afford anybody to cut the grass, my son-in-law does it for me, but he was so polite, seemed like a real nice boy, I was sorry I had to turn him down. So then he says could he trouble me for a drink of water, ma'am, and I naturally said, why, surely, sonny, and let him in, and the next thing I knew he pulled this knife— But he was just a little kid! Just a boy, didn't look more than twelve years old!" She had given them a description, such as it was: a light-colored Negro boy about that age, maybe five-six, slightly built. Mrs. Walker had definitely been raped, said the doctor, and cut about with a knife. She had been surprised: cops weren't much, any more.

The second victim, last week, had been Miss Ruth Trimball who lived alone in a rented house two blocks down the street from Mrs. Walker. She was sixty-eight, still worked at a drugstore over on Jefferson, and had just got home from work when a boy rang her doorbell and asked if she wanted anybody to do yard work. She told the same story Mrs. Walker had—such a nice polite boy, she hadn't thought twice about letting him in, for his drink of water. She'd been raped and cut too, and gave the same description.

Yesterday Mrs. Wilma Lightner had called LAPD and reported finding her mother injured when she went to see her. Mrs. Sylvia Beaver had been raped and knifed, according to the hospital, but would recover. Piggott and Schenke, on night watch, had taken a statement from Mrs. Lightner last night. Her mother was a widow, sixty-two, owned her own home on Twenty-third Street, was living on Social Security.

Landers came back to report that the hospital said Mrs. Beaver could be questioned. "Take your car," he added, "that thing's acting up on me—I'm going to have to figure on a new one." And what with Phil talking about new furniture—he and Policewoman Phil O'Neill had just got married last August, and Landers was discovering all the fallacies of that one about two living as cheaply as one. The Corvair was of an age to be retired, and with Phil so enthusiastic about her little Gremlin he'd rather like to try one of his own, but the payments—

They took Grace's car, the little blue racing Elva. At

the hospital, they found Mrs. Beaver propped up in bed with her daughter in attendance. She was a fat, black, very respectable-looking matron with round steel-rimmed spectacles, and she looked at the detectives indignantly.

"Tell you? I can most certainly tell you all about it!" she said loudly. "I was never so surprised in my life! He was just a little kid—a little boy! Rang the bell and asked to cut my lawn for a dollar. I told him I didn't need anybody to cut the grass, but he seemed like a nice youngster, so polite and all, and when he asked for a drink of water, I didn't see any harm in letting him in—"

She gave them the same description. It amounted to assault with intent, like the other ones.

"Offbeat all right," said Grace on the way back to headquarters. And of course there was no lead on it at all. They could look in Records for the description, but it was general.

At the office, Hackett was in talking to Mendoza, and as they came in Lake told Grace and Landers that there was a new body reported by the Fire Department. Glasser and Palliser had gone out on it.

"There's nothing in it," said Hackett. "I gave it an hour or two—just to look—and it's silly. This Yeager is letting his imagination run wild or something. Overheard a joke and built it up. These Lamperts are ordinary quiet people, the son's on full disability from a service injury, and by what I heard from the people I talked to in the apartment, they get on just fine together."

"Yes," said Mendoza inattentively, and pulled the trigger on his flame-thrower.

"That damned thing," said Hackett. "Set the place afire if you're not careful."

"Don't be silly, Arturo." The phone buzzed on his

desk and he picked it up. "Robbery-Homicide, Mendoza."

Without preamble, Dr. Bainbridge said crisply in his ear, "Traffic sent in a body on Monday night, said to be a hit-run victim. What it looked like. It isn't. Man about thirty, a heavy drinker, and he was beaten to death with a club or something similar. I thought you'd like to know."

"Hell and damnation!" said Mendoza.

TWO

PALLISER WENT OUT with Glasser on the new call, and condescended to fold his six feet into the little Gremlin Glasser had so luckily won in a drawing last year. As Glasser backed out of the slot Palliser massaged his handsome straight nose in a habitual gesture and said, "You know, I'll have to do something about that dog, damn it."

"What dog? Oh, the pup that woman gave you?"

"That one," said Palliser. "She's a very nice dog, Trina, but she's big, and going to be bigger. A German shepherd after all. She ought to have obedience training, but damn it, how can I take her? Robin can't, with the baby. I've been on the phone to this local club, and the nearest class to us is Saturday afternoons, and I'm only off on Monday. This fellow said I could get a book and try training her myself, just a few minutes a day, but I don't know."

Glasser hadn't any useful suggestions.

The new call turned out to be an old building out on San Pedro, plastered with CONDEMNED signs and looking ready to fall down, all four stories of it. The fire truck was still there, and the battalion chief waiting for them. "Not much of a fire," he told them, "but when we'd knocked it down we found the body. Somebody likely thought he'd get rid of it by lighting a match, but he bungled the job, this damp weather."

"Arson?" said Glasser. "Definitely?"

"You better believe. A trail of kerosene to the body, but it fizzled out—you notice it's a derelict building, part of the roof's gone and there was a mist this morning. It's back here." Even on this gray morning threatening rain, a little crowd had gathered to watch the activity, and the uniformed men from the black and white were keeping them back. The chief led Glasser and Palliser into what might have started life as a small hotel fifty years ago, and ended up as an apartment house. The place had been a shambles even before the fire; there were clusters of broken bricks and heaps of plaster dust, gaping empty doorways, and most of it was open to the sky. "The quake in seventy-one finished it off, but they just haven't got round to taking the rest of it down. There you are." The chief pointed unnecessarily.

Near what had been the rear door of the building, between the empty doorway and another pile of rubbled brick, the body sprawled almost casually. Palliser and Glasser didn't need the chief's interpretation to read what had likely happened here. It was a little, slender body, and somebody had tried to set fire to it, but the fire had gone out without doing much damage.

"A lot of smoke," said the chief. "Fellow at the tailor shop down the block called in the alarm." There was a cluster of miscellaneous little shops down the block, in other ramshackle buildings not yet condemned—the cluster of citizens outside had probably come from there.

Palliser squatted over the body. "Make any educated guesses, Henry?"

"One," said Glasser sadly. "She was raped—assaulted at least—and probably strangled."

Palliser grunted. "You'd better call up S.I.D. Go through the motions, photographs and so on." Glasser went out to use the radio in the black and white.

The body was that of a young girl: very young, Palliser thought. Dark blonde, thin, hard to say if she'd been pretty or not, the face discolored with death or the effects of strangulation, the body already stiff: dead awhile. She was naked from the waist down, and there was dark dried blood on the inside of her thin little-girl thighs. Still on the upper half of the body was a pale-green knit turtleneck sweater, pulled up to show part of a dirty white brassiere; by the slight small swell of one breast, she'd hardly needed that. On her feet were what looked like new sneakers, blue and white, fairly clean, and white ankle socks. One arm was flung out from the body, and Palliser had just made a couple of discoveries when Glasser came back.

"The mobile lab's on the way."

"Good. Look at this," said Palliser. "Makes it not quite so anonymous, at least. We may get her identified right off."

"Oh, yes," said Glasser, squatting beside him. "Helpful."

The trail of kerosene had led from the front hallway, but the fire had first created a lot of smoke, and according to the engine boys had been already dying out when they got here; it hadn't damaged the body at all. On the outflung bare arm on the inside of the elbow, clearly visible, was a long puckered scar; on the third finger of that hand was a ring. Palliser had delicately manipulated the nearly rigid wrist around to inspect the bezel. "We'll want pictures, but it could make shortcuts all right." The ring was a school ring, the usual indecipherable crest, a little blue enamel, and in minute letters around that, FRESNO JR. HIGH. Palliser stood up.

"Fresno," said Glasser. "My God, these kids. She doesn't look over thirteen or fourteen. And ending up down here—" But it wasn't anything new, they'd seen much the same thing before, and there wasn't much to say about it.

They waited for the mobile lab, told Duke to get shots of the ring and send it up to the office. It was getting on for noon then. In the Missing Persons office back at headquarters they found Lieutenant Carey hunched over a report, and he just groaned at mention of a possibly-reported-missing juvenile.

"We've got a million of 'em, from all over the country. Take your pick."

"Maybe we can narrow it down," said Palliser. "I don't think this one was very far into the teens. An older one, she could have been out roaming on her own a couple of years, but one this young—she might not have been away from home and mother very long. And we've got two good leads—she had on a ring from Fresno Junior High, and there's a distinctive scar on the left arm."

"We can have a look at the recent files," said Carey. They did. Just in the last month, enough juveniles had been reported missing to this office to build up those files into a thick stack, and they had to be glanced at one by one, the description scanned briefly to weed it out. Palliser and Glasser took a lunch break, ran into Galeano and Conway at Federico's on North Broadway, and heard about the offbeat case Carey had just handed them. Glasser went down to S.I.D. when they got back to base, to see if they'd come up with anything, and Palliser went back to the files. It was after two-thirty when he came up with a recently filed report that rang bells.

Reported missing to the Fresno police, Sandra Moseley, aged fifteen, five-two, a hundred and five, blonde and blue: scar inside left arm, appendectomy scar; reported by mother, Mrs. Anita Moseley. She was thought to have been with another girl, Stephanie Peacock, also fifteen, also missing.

"Kids," thought Palliser. He went back up to Robbery-Homicide and got on the phone to the Fresno department. A Captain Almont said he'd get in touch with Mrs. Moseley. "It looks pretty definite, it's this Moseley girl dead down there?"

"Well, we'd like a positive identification, but there's the ring and the scar. No autopsy yet, but it looks pretty certain for Murder One."

"Hell of a thing," said Almont. "We'll get in touch with the mother and get back to you."

"Thanks very much," said Palliser. He wondered momentarily what had happened to the other girl—if they had been together. He wondered what he was going to do about Trina. The obedience club secretary had given him the name of a book to get.

Glasser came back and said S.I.D. hadn't picked up any latents or any other physical evidence at the scene. She'd probably been killed elsewhere and brought there just before the fire was set. "Well, we've probably got her identified, at least," said Palliser absently.

Galeano and Conway had been deflected onto the supposed hit-run, which everybody had comfortably supposed would get buried in Pending. Landers had gone to cover the inquest.

At least they had no sooner been informed that it wasn't a hit-run than they got an I.D. for him. Traffic had come across the body about midnight on Monday, in the middle of Valencia Avenue up from Venice Boulevard; there hadn't been any I.D. on it, so the lab had collected his prints next morning to run through. Ten minutes after

Bainbridge had called Mendoza, the routine report came in. His prints were in their records; he had a small pedigree from a while back. He was Robert Chard, now thirty-nine. He'd been picked up for auto theft as a juvenile, for attempted assault just after he'd turned legally adult, and had one count of B. and E. after that. He'd never served any time at all, and apparently had never been in trouble since.

The latest address was sixteen years out of date, but it was a place to start. Longwood Avenue. You had to go by routine even when it looked unproductive. Not feeling very hopeful, Galeano tried that address, which was an old frame house in need of paint, and turned up a Mrs. Holly, a thirtyish slattern who said she was Robert Chard's sister.

"Why you looking for Bob? He hasn't been in any trouble for a long time, nor he won't be either, under the thumb of that bitch he married. You cops tryin' to make out he done something?"

"No, ma'am," said Galeano politely. "We'd like to get his body identified. He's dead."

"Well, for God's sake," she said mildly. "Bob? Is that so? Was it an accident?"

"We're not sure," said Galeano. "When did you see him last?"

"Gee, I'd hafta think. The last years, since he got married, rest of the family hardly ever saw him at all. That bitch, she used to be scared he'd spend money on presents for Ma, and he kinda got out of the habit of coming—of course Ma died last year— Well, I could tell you where they were living, last I knew, but I don't know if they still lived there. It was Constance Street. My God, think of Bob dead—damn, I s'pose I got to get in touch with her, I oughta go to the funeral."

If you didn't get rich at a cop's job, Galeano reflected, you had a box seat at the eternal spectacle of human nature in action.

Nobody was home at the address on Constance, an old cracker-box duplex. A nameplate next to the doorbell had a hand-printed slip in it that said CHARD, so at least this was the right place. Funny, maybe nobody had missed him yet. Or maybe nobody cared whether he came home or not. Galeano tried the neighbors, and found only one home, a deaf elderly man who told him that Mis' Chard worked someplace uptown, and he didn't take any notice when she usually came home.

Better leave a note for the night watch to contact her, thought Galeano.

He was still intrigued by the empty wheelchair in that tale Carey had spun them, and he wanted to talk to that blonde, start asking questions around on that; but what with all the legwork, it was the middle of the afternoon and he still had to type out a report on this.

He got home about six-thirty, to his neat small bachelor apartment on Edgemont up in Hollywood, rummaged in the freezer and put a TV dinner in the oven, and sat down with the *Herald* over a glass of the cheap red wine he liked. His mother and sisters had given up years ago deviling him to find a nice girl and get married; at thirty-six, Galeano had settled into comfortable bachelorhood.

That was a fishy little story of Carey's, he thought idly. It would be interesting to know what really had happened there, just how Edwin Fleming had managed to melt into thin air, leaving his empty wheelchair behind. Galeano thought that blonde couldn't be quite so dumb as Carey thought.

Mendoza was greeted exuberantly by the twins as he came in the back door, and Mrs. MacTaggart rescued him.

"Your father'll come to see you in your baths, my lambs, right now you'll let him have some peace and quiet." She led them off firmly.

He found Alison, surrounded by the four cats Bast, Sheba, Nefertite and El Señor, stretched out on the sectional in the front room, with Cedric curled up on the floor beside them. "Hello, *amado*," said Alison. "I'm sorry I was cross this morning, but this is turning out to be quite a project. No, I don't want any dinner—I had some bouillon a while ago, Mairí bullied it down me—but she's getting something for you. And if you're going to have a drink first, you can bring me just a little crème de menthe to settle my insides." She looked wan.

At his first touch on the cupboard door where the liquor was kept, El Señor appeared, his Siamese mask-in-reverse wearing a hopeful look. Mendoza poured him half an ounce of rye in a saucer and took his own drink and Alison's back to the living room.

"You know, Luis," she said, half sitting up to take the glass, "we'll have to think about a new house. Just as I was saying last night. Because there are only four bedrooms here, and with the baby we'll need five. And besides—"

"One thing," said Mendoza, "leading to another. *Pues qué.*" The twins had been, not without protest, graduated to separate rooms.

"And it did seem like a lot of space at first, two lots," said Alison, sipping, "but it isn't really enough room for Cedric—he needs more exercise. And I've been thinking, it'd be nice to be—you know—a little farther out, on an acre or even more—it isn't as if you haven't got the money."

"Delusions of grandeur," said Mendoza.

"Well, we might as well enjoy it while we can. I think I feel better," said Alison. "Give me a cigarette, darling.

You might tell Mairí I could take some mushroom soup." The phone rang down the hall and he went to answer it, passing El Señor thoughtfully licking his whiskers.

"Mendoza."

It was the main desk at headquarters; the night watch wasn't on yet, upstairs. Central Receiving had just called in the information that Father O'Brien had died an hour ago. "Thanks so much," said Mendoza.

So the pretty boys had a homicide to their credit now. And still not a smell of a lead as to where to look for them.

Just before Palliser left the office, Fresno called back. Mrs. Moseley had been contacted and would come down to L.A. tomorrow to look at the body.

"The report we had, they thought there was another girl with the Moseley girl," said Almont. "You just found the one?"

"We think. Just her so far," said Palliser. "Thanks, we'll be expecting her."

"No trouble. These kids. Poor woman sounded all broken up."

Palliser stopped at a big bookstore in Hollywood on his way home and asked for a copy of *The Kennel Club Obedience Manual*. He handed over seven bucks for it and had it under his arm when he unlocked the driveway gate and slid through it. A solid object weighing some seventy pounds immediately hit him amidships like a bomb, and he said breathlessly, "Down, girl!" But she impeded every step to the back door and into the kitchen, giving him to understand what a hard day she'd had guarding the family every alert minute, all for love of him. In the kitchen, she rose up lovingly at Roberta and nearly knocked her over. She was, no question, going to be a very large German shepherd; only nine months now and still growing.

"We'll have to do something about training her, John," said Roberta severely.

"I know, I know. I've got a book," said Palliser, and then discovered that Trina had it instead, chewing the cover like a bone. He rescued it hastily and hoped that wasn't a bad omen.

Piggott and Schenke came on night watch at the same time and shared an elevator. It was Shogart's night off. Piggott didn't mind doing a tour of night watch, except that it interfered with choir practice and Prudence didn't like it, but he'd have a chance to shift back in three months. Schenke had been on night watch so long he'd come to prefer it.

Galeano had left them a note to call this Mrs. Chard, tell her her husband was dead. Schenke tried the number and got a busy signal. They'd try again.

At seven-thirty they got a call from Traffic, a new body. Looking, said Traffic, like Murder One. "The citizens keep us busy, Matt," said Schenke.

"Or Satan does," said Piggott. They were on the way out when the phone buzzed again, and he went back to pick it up. "Robbery-Homicide, Detective Piggott."

"Oh—is Sergeant Palliser there? That's the name I was told to—"

"Sergeant Palliser's on day watch, ma'am. Can I help you?" The woman sounded upset.

"I—yes, I suppose. It's just to let him know—that is, whoever's concerned—I'm Mrs. Moseley. In Fresno. They think—the police here said—you think you've found my daughter there. D-dead. I was to come— But just now— just a while ago—the Peacocks called me—"

"You want me to give this to Sergeant Palliser?" asked Piggott patiently.

"Yes, if you would. We were sure they were together, Sandra and Stephanie. Ran away together. And Mrs. Peacock just c-called to say—they've heard from Stephanie. They're driving down there to meet her, she wants to come home, and I'm coming with them. Because if Stephanie's all right, maybe it's all a mistake and the dead girl isn't Sandra —but—"

"I'll pass it on to Palliser, ma'am." Piggott hadn't heard anything about the dead girl; he scrawled that down as she hung up with a gasp, and put the note on Palliser's desk.

The address for the new body was Orchard Street, a little backwater of old single houses, a few duplexes, past Virgil. The black and white was in front of one of the singles, a little white frame house looking shabby. The uniformed men were talking to a paunchy shaken-looking man at the curb.

"These are the detectives, Mr. Buford. Mr. Piggott, Mr. Schenke. You tell it all to them. It's inside," added one of the Traffic men. "Looks like a B. and E. and assault for robbery. Maybe somebody didn't expect him to be home."

"That's why I got worried," said the paunchy man. "Dick usually was home—he's a great homebody, and he was between jobs, see, I told you that, he's in construction and they can't work this weather, but it didn't matter to Dick, he's got savings, makes good money, and besides he don't buy much for himself—he just lost his wife last year and it kind of took the heart out of him, they hadn't any kids, and I used to call him three, four times a week, just to talk—oh, I didn't tell you fellows, Dick's my brother —I'm Robert—we were always kind of close—and I couldn't raise him on the phone no way, the last three days, and I got worried about it, maybe he was sick or something, because he's not one for going out much, maybe once a month he'll go up to a neighborhood bar for a couple of beers, but not regular—and I said to my wife, I got to find out if anything's wrong, and I drove up right after work. I live way out past Thousand Oaks and it was murder on the freeway but I—" He stopped, gulped, and said, "Murder! Dick! But who'd murder Dick? A quiet fellow like Dick! It don't make sense!"

"He had a key to the house, went in and found him and called us," said the Traffic man, sounding tired.

Piggott and Schenke went up the narrow front walk. The front door was open, past a neatly mended screen door. The body was in the middle of the living room, a small square room crowded with old-fashioned furniture, a big TV console in one corner. A straight chair was over-turned, the carpet rucked up in folds, a clock and vase from an overturned table lying around the corpse; there'd been some sort of scuffle here. The TV was on, volume turned low.

The body was lying face up in the middle of the room, a big fleshy middle-aged man with a Roman nose and a mop of gray hair. They looked at him and Schenke said, "He was in a fight all right, probably right here. Could be he hit his head on something, or the other guy hit him de-liberately to kill. We can ask the brother what's missing. We better get S.I.D. out for pictures and so on."

They called up the lab boys and talked to Robert Buford while they waited. He said his brother Dick was kind of a loner, didn't have too many friends; trouble was he and Mary, his wife, had been awful close, didn't seem to want anybody else, and when she died— Since then, when Dick wasn't working, he mostly stayed home, watched TV. He didn't have any worries about money, they owned the house; Dick was kind of close with money.

When the lab men had taken pictures and printed the body, they went over him. In one pocket there was seventeen cents, a handkerchief, what looked like car keys, and an empty wallet. There was an old Chevy in the garage, Buford's car, undisturbed. They asked Robert about what cash Dick might have carried, and he said helplessly, "Jesus, I don't know what to say, I don't know how much he might have had—could be he'd just run out and was figuring to go to the bank tomorrow, or he coulda had a bundle and been robbed—I don't know." He peered sorrowfully at the dead man. "You don't figure he coulda just had a heart attack or something? He was fifty-nine. No, I suppose it wasn't."

The autopsy would tell them, but they'd both seen enough bodies to have an educated guess about this.

It would give the day watch something else to work.

Hackett was off on Thursdays. "Thank heaven," said Angel, getting out her car keys, "there's one day I can go to the market without the kids. But I'm going to see Alison first. Poor darling, she's feeling awful with this one so far— I think it was a mistake myself—"

"I'm taking bets it'll be a redhead," said Hackett.

"And, Art—if you touch a crumb of that cream pie I'll kill you. You're ten pounds up again."

"All right, all right." But after she'd backed out, he listened to Mark prattle about school—Mark would be starting kindergarten next month, which seemed impossible —and thought, It was probably something like that. Whatever that Yeager had overheard, or thought he had. People said things, I'll kill you, It was murder—and also made jokes. What they didn't do, at least people like these Lam-

perts, from what he'd gathered about them, was casually
plan a real killing with the apartment door open and
people wandering around.

He called in after a while, keeping an eye on his darling Sheila trotting busily around, to hear if anything new
had gone down. Lake told him that that priest had died,
about the dead teenager, and the new one last night. So
that unholy trio had done a murder now; Hackett wished
there was some way to get a lead to them.

The first thing Mendoza did on Thursday morning was
to get on to S.I.D. as to what, if anything, they'd got on
that Pontiac.

"We've been busy," said Duke. "I was just getting out
a report. Nothing. The priest's prints were in it, and that
other priest's, he used it sometimes—but that's all. If he
was jumped around there, it was before he got into the car.
No, we didn't turn up any keys anywhere."

"Thanks so much for nothing." But there *was* a little
something there, Mendoza thought, and said so to Higgins
who had just come in, looming as bulkily as Hackett.

"What?" asked Higgins. "I don't see anything, Luis."

"Like the dog that didn't bark in the night, George.
O'Brien dropped the keys when they jumped him, but they
didn't take the car. I know we've got *nada absolutamente*
on these louts, as far as court evidence goes, but a picture
builds in my mind." Jason Grace had wandered in, Landers
and Conway behind him, and Galeano; they listened to the
boss having a hunch. "The fancy clothes," said Mendoza,
picking up the flame-thrower lighter and pointing it absently at Higgins, who shied back. "And one of the victims
—a woman—said that one of them, she thinks the tall
blond one, called her a dirty peasant. Which is not the kind
of—mmh—invective you hear around Temple Street, boys.

And they couldn't be bothered to steal a ten-year-old Pontiac. I get the feeling they're not native to our beat."

"Then what the hell are they doing down here, jumping the senior citizens?" said Higgins. "For kicks?"

"Es posible," said Mendoza. He pressed the trigger, the flame shot out and he lit his cigarette. "They haven't made any kind of haul. Any halfway smart four-year-old around here would know that the average senior citizen in this area isn't exactly loaded, or he wouldn't still be living in the area. It's possible our pretty boys in their fancy clothes—from somewhere a little way up the social scale—are prowling around here just for the kicks, beating up the senior citizens for fun. Mmh. *Cómo no*—maybe with the idea that cops wouldn't go to much trouble over these particular senior citizens."

"That's a little far out," said Higgins, "or is it?"

"He smells these things," said Grace seriously. "I'll add, what you might call a mixed population down here. One of these here racists, Loo-tenant suh?"

Mendoza laughed. "I don't know if I smell anything or not, Jase. Just off the top of my mind, if I remember right, two of the victims were Mexican, three black, the rest just people—and O'Brien. They must have seen his priest's collar—but it was dark. But—*¡vaya historia!*—that 'dirty peasant' sticks in my mind. Not Temple Street. More like U.C.L.A."

"Which may be a thought, but it doesn't take us anywhere to look," said Conway. "Have you had a chance to look at the offbeat thing Carey handed us? I like it, as a story, but it's going to be a lot of work for nothing. I want to see that blonde."

Mendoza picked up the night report, didn't start reading it. "You'll tell me about it. A blonde?"

"I'm bound to say," said Galeano, "it's the wheelchair

that sort of caught my imagination—the empty wheelchair. You can see what Carey means—it's a locked-room puzzle in a sort of way."

"An empty wheelchair," said Mendoza, cigarette suspended. "So, I'll hear about it."

Sergeant Lake looked in. "There's a Mrs. Chard here and some other people. A Mrs. Moseley and a Mr. and Mrs. Peacock asking for Palliser."

"So the night watch got hold of the Chard woman," said Galeano. "I'd better talk to her, Jimmy. John hasn't showed up yet. You can tell the boss about the wheelchair, Rich."

Mrs. Cecelia Chard identified the body with loud sobs and groans. She was a thin dark hard-faced woman with shrewish black eyes, and Galeano didn't take to her at all. She was supported by her mother, Mrs. Wilma Dixon, and her brother Elmer, both generally resembling her.

"Poor Bob," she lamented, drying her eyes with a Coty-scented handkerchief when they'd got back from the morgue and Galeano had settled them down in the office to make a statement. "Like I said, Mr. Galeano, I never reported him missing because I thought he was off on a bender, like he did every now 'n' then, and goodness knows Mother and Elmer can bear me out. I'm not about to say he was the best husband in the world, Mr. Galeano, but I wouldn't have wished him a terrible death like that—he must've got into a fight with somebody when he was drunk. I got to say, he used to get fighting mad with any liquor in him, it takes some like that, you know."

"A regular mean man in drink he was, all right," said Elmer, and giggled.

"He certainly was," said Mrs. Dixon with a long sigh.

"It's a sorry thing he should've come to such a bad end, but running around with riffraff the way he did, in all them bars, no wonder. I'm sorry to say it, Mr. Galeano, but I guess my girl's rid of a bad bargain."

Galeano didn't think much of them at all, but there was the one about birds of a feather. Their estimation of Chard was probably right. He'd been found about half a block down the side street from a bar on the corner of Venice Boulevard, and it was very likely he'd got into a brawl with some other drunks and died of it. It was just more of the sordid violence cops got paid to cope with, and it made him feel tired.

He got the gist of that down in a statement, and Mrs. Chard signed it. He told them they'd be notified when the body could be released, and they thanked him and went away.

And he supposed that somebody ought to ask a few questions at that bar, try to find out who the other drunks were—not that it seemed very important.

Mendoza scanned the night report before he listened to Conway, and handed the Buford thing to Landers and Grace. It didn't look as if there'd be much handle to it, unless S.I.D. turned up something.

Then he heard all about Carey's blonde and the empty wheelchair, and like Galeano he was fascinated. Luis Rodolfo Vicente Mendoza was not, perhaps, temperamentally suited to be a cop, who by the nature of the job had to deal with physical evidence, facts and figures and tangibilities. The men who worked with him were convinced that his natural calling was that of a cardsharp, that most innocent of con-men who relied on instinctive knowledge of human nature.

"I see what Carey means," he said amusedly. "Masterly

gall. Please, sir, he's gone, I don't know where. But the empty wheelchair—which was probably quite inadvertent, if we're reading it right—it's a nice touch. *¡Me gusta!*"

"So all we do is find the boyfriend," said Conway. "I thought Carey'd made kind of heavy weather of it. In spite of the—er—imaginative touch, it looks open and shut to me."

Mendoza regarded him sardonically. "Yes and no, Rich. In this job, ninety-nine times out of a hundred, things are just exactly what they look like. Just occasionally they aren't. But I want a look at Carey's blonde and the wheelchair. That so eloquently empty wheelchair!"

"So does Nick. But there's only one obvious answer, isn't there?"

"Es posible," said Mendoza. "Go see if he's back from the morgue."

Palliser had got caught in a jam on the freeway, a pileup backed up for a mile, and it was nearly nine o'clock when he came into the office to find four forlorn-looking people waiting to see him. Mrs. Anita Moseley, Mr. and Mrs. Simon Peacock, and Stephanie Peacock.

Mr. Peacock offered to go to the morgue to make the identification. "I knew Sandra all her life, since she and Stephanie started school together. I wish you'd let me, Anita—save you the agony—" But Mrs. Moseley said tautly she had to see for herself and be sure. She was a nice-looking woman, late thirties, brown hair, good figure, conservatively dressed. They were all nice people, Palliser could see, in the euphemistic phrase: upright middle-class people: Peacock an insurance agent, the two women ladies.

At the morgue, Mrs. Moseley looked at the body and said thinly, "Yes, that's Sandra. That's her. Oh, my God, to have it all end like this—I tried so hard— To see her like that— No, I'm all right. Honestly, I'm all right. But when it was all for nothing—no reason for her to—"

Back at the office, Palliser got Wanda Larsen in for support, and she was briskly sympathetic but businesslike, their very efficient policewoman; Mrs. Moseley talked mostly to her, and Wanda took unobtrusive notes.

"I have to say, she—Sandra—had been more and more difficult—since the divorce," she said painfully. "You see, I divorced her father last year. He—that doesn't matter, the reasons, but you see he'd always spoiled her dreadfully, and I'm afraid—she's just a child really, she didn't understand about the divorce, she always idolized her father and I didn't want to—to destroy any of that— maybe that was a mistake, if I had told her—but I guess that doesn't matter now either. I tried to discipline her— sensibly—God knows I tried. But—"

They listened patiently, asked questions. When Sandra hadn't come home, last Saturday, she had called the Pea- cocks first. "Because Sandra and Stephanie were always together, best friends, and I thought—" And Stephanie hadn't come home either. By next day it was pretty clear they'd run away together: some of their clothes were miss- ing. "Oh, I've got to say it," said Mrs. Moseley, "Sandra would have been the leader, she always was—" She'd gone to the police then.

The Peacocks said that, of course, they'd been frantic, their only daughter missing, and then she'd phoned them last night. She was in a big railroad station in L.A. with no money—scared and sorry and wanting to come home. "We told her just to stay there, we'd come as soon as we could," said Mrs. Peacock. "And we called Anita—"

"If you'd called us," said Wanda, "we'd have taken care of her until you got here, Mrs. Peacock."

"Well, we don't know anything about the police.

Naturally. We just wanted to get here and find her. And thank God she's all right—when I think what could have happened—that wild headstrong girl—I'm sorry, Anita, but you know she was, you tried but you know yourself—"

Mrs. Moseley sobbed once, convulsively, and Wanda brought her a glass of water.

"Well, now, Stephanie," said Palliser, wishing he knew more about teenagers, "suppose you tell us what you know about this."

She was a thin, gawky girl, not terribly pretty and looking even younger than she was, with long brown stringy hair and mild brown eyes; right now she was scared. "I—I—I didn't really want to—it was all Sandra! I was scared all the time, but Sandra—"

"My poor darling!" said her mother.

Peacock had better sense. "Now listen here, young lady," he said roughly. "If you were scared it was your own damn fault for being such a little fool. You speak up and tell whatever you know right now!"

"Y-yes, Daddy. I'm sorry. I w-will," gulped Stephanie unsteadily.

THREE

"I DIDN'T WANT to, it was Sandra," began Stephanie nervously. "She said—she said her mother was so strict and old-fashioned and she'd—she'd treated her father awful bad, she didn't want to, you know, stay with her any more and—" She stopped and looked uneasily at Mrs. Moseley, her parents, and stuck there. Mrs. Peacock cast a somewhat unloving look at Mrs. Moseley, and Wanda intervened smoothly.

It might be better, she suggested, if they just left Stephanie to her and Sergeant Palliser; it was likely to be a long business taking a statement, and she'd be right with Stephanie all the time, they might be asking her to look at some photographs. Peacock said that was a good idea, they'd heard enough of it that he didn't want to hear it all again, and he wasn't going to face that drive again until tomorrow. Mrs. Moseley said faintly she'd just like to go back to the motel and lie down. Peacock exchanged a look with Palliser and urged his wife, protesting, to the door. "I guess we can leave it to you. We're at the Holiday Inn off the Hollywood freeway."

"What would we do without you, lady?" said Palliser to Wanda, and meant it.

"All part of the job. . . . Now, Stephanie, you can

say whatever you want to us, you know, we won't mind," she said comfortably. "We want to know anything you can tell us that might help to find out what happened to Sandra."

"You're a policewoman, aren't you? I guess that must be kind of an interesting job. Well, I know that. It's all just so *awful*—Sandra *dead* and all—but I want to tell how it was, only Mama and Daddy carried on so, and I didn't like to say in front of Sandra's mother—"

"That's all right now, you just tell it the way it happened."

"She said awful things about her mother," said Sandra miserably, "but maybe they were so, I don't know. She said we could go to L.A., Hollywood, and get jobs, school was stupid and all the teachers squares and silly. She wanted to be a model, she said maybe we could get jobs like that right away, or there are schools where you can learn. I—well, I didn't want to, I like school all right, but Sandra—she could always make me go along, sort of. She'd done it other times too. And her mother works, since the divorce, and my mother had a club meeting—last Saturday, I mean, so that's when we did it. I packed a lot of clothes and things in Mama's biggest suitcase, and Sandra had an overnight bag and a plane case, and we just took the bus out the state highway. It was crowded and nobody paid any notice, and at the end of the line we—uh—got out and, you know, started to hitch." She took a breath. "I was scared right from the first, that's a thing you're never supposed to do, get in strange cars, but Sandra wasn't afraid of anything ever. She had fifteen dollars she'd saved from her allowance and I had nearly eight."

Palliser and Wanda refrained from looking at each other. Glasser wandered in and pulled up a chair behind

Palliser silently. She hardly noticed him; she was talking to Wanda.

"Well, this man gave us a ride all the way to L.A. He was a salesman of some kind, he was nice and friendly, he joked with Sandra—she told him we were both eighteen and I guess he believed that. She said we were going to see some relatives of hers here and just to let us out at Hollywood Boulevard, that was the only name here we knew, and he did. He said, Hollywood and what, and we didn't know what to say." Palliser put out one cigarette, lit another, and thought, People. "But it was all so *queer,* sort of," said Stephanie, still sounding surprised. "Not what we thought it'd be—not what we thought Hollywood'd be like! Just a great big city, and Woolworth's and Penney's and drugstores just like home, only some funnier-looking people—I mean, it wasn't glamorous or anything at all! And we had some sandwiches at a place, but it was Sunday and no place was open, I mean we looked in the yellow pages for those model agencies like Sandra said, but they wouldn't be open till Monday and I said where were we going to sleep. And then Sandra got talking to this man—"

"Sunday," said Wanda. "The man who drove you here, that was over Saturday night? Do you know his name?"

"He said to call him Jim, that's all. Yes, ma'am, we drove all night, he bought us two sandwiches at a place on the way. And this other man Sandra got talking to, it was at this place on Hollywood Boulevard we went in to eat. I mean, I didn't like it, but a person doesn't know what to *do,*" said Stephanie, blinking back sudden tears. "My mother doesn't think black people are very nice at all and Daddy always says nonsense, you judge people as individuals, and at school they seem to think they're better than us because of slavery and all that and how do you know, anyway— But I *didn't* like him! He got talking to Sandra and she told him about going to be a model and get jobs here and he said maybe he could help. He said did we have any place to stay and Sandra said not yet, and so he said we could stay at his place, his wife'd be glad to have us—I didn't want to go, even when he said that, but Sandra said not to be silly. And he had a car, he took us to this house."

"Did he tell you his name? What did he look like?"

"Sure. His name was Steve Smith. I didn't see how he might help us get jobs, because, you know, he talked— oh, real ignorant and bad grammar. But after, Sandra said maybe he was a servant to somebody real high up in the movies or something like that. Anyway, he took us to this house, but his wife wasn't there and he said she must've gone someplace."

"Did you notice the name of the street?" asked Palliser.

She shook her head. "It wasn't a very good neighborhood, I guess—lots of narrow little streets and awful run-down old houses. There wasn't much furniture there, just some chairs and a TV and a couple of beds. And he went and got some hamburgers and asked would we like a couple of joints, and Sandra said sure but I knew that was marijuana and I was scared to because of what the school nurse told us last semester, so I didn't take any but Sandra— Oh, what he looked like. Well, he was kind of tall, as tall as you anyway," she said, looking at Palliser, "and not very black, just sort of medium, and he had a mustache and a funny little beard just at the end of his chin."

"What about the car?" asked Wanda.

"I don't know the—the brand. It was an old car, a two-door. Blue, I guess. Anyway, Sandra got to talking real silly and I was scared then but I didn't know what to do, I just went in the bedroom and shut the door. I guess I went to sleep. And all next day he was gone someplace and we mostly watched TV. There were Cokes and a lot of stuff to eat there, only by then I—just—wanted—to— go home!" said Stephanie. "And he came back that night and said he'd been talking to somebody he knew about jobs for us, and so Sandra said wait and see. But the next night when he came, he got to talking sort of, you know, dirty, and tried to fool around with Sandra and I got more scared and I ran out the back door without my suitcase or anything, and I just about died till it got light—only I didn't know where I was or what to do—I had my wallet in my pocket, I still had about four dollars and some change, and pretty soon I found that big public library, I felt sort of safe there and it was warm, but it closed at six and I just sort of walked on and I wanted to go home just the *worst way,* and so when I found that big railroad station I knew what to do. There were public phones and I got the operator and said to reverse the charges, and called home, and Daddy *swore* at me the minute he heard my voice, I guess he'd been awful scared about me. But I bet he couldn't have been as scared as I was."

And with reason, thought Palliser. Kids! If she was immature for her age—unlike the other one—still it was a funny age, a mixture of emotion and ignorance. She'd been lucky to be scared enough to run. "It was Tuesday night when you left Sandra there, wherever it was?" That fitted in; the state of the body yesterday morning, she had probably been killed Tuesday night.

"Yes, sir."

"Do you think you could recognize the house where he took you? Did you notice any street names when you ran away?"

She shook her head. "It was dark. Oh, I remember one, Flower Street, just before I came to the library."

Palliser rubbed his nose. That wasn't much help; by what she said, she could have walked three dozen blocks before that. What was in his mind was that city dwellers tend to be curiously insular, stick to their own little corners: and when Steve Smith attempted to get rid of the body in that derelict building, a hundred to one he lived somewhere nearby, or had lived there. A house. Well, there were enough old streets with ramshackle old houses along them, both sides of San Pedro and other main drags down there.

"Do you think you could recognize him, Stephanie?" asked Wanda. "If you saw his photograph?"

Stephanie nodded doubtfully. "I think so. I tried to make Sandra come with me, I just knew something awful'd happen if we stayed there, but you never could get Sandra to do things. She got *you* to do things. Only—when Mama told me what happened to her—I mean, I knew Sandra all my life." But this time, in spite of everything, Stephanie was rather enjoying herself, all of them listening to every word and Wanda taking notes.

"Well, I'll tell you," said Palliser, looking at his watch, "suppose Miss Larsen takes you to lunch, Stephanie, and then we'll take a ride around and see if you recognize any buildings, and then you can look at some pictures."

She agreed almost enjoyably. When Wanda had led her out, Palliser looked at Glasser and said, "Terrifying, no? Kids."

"She was lucky," agreed Glasser sleepily. "Does Harry

sound like the kind to have a whole house of his own? Even a ramshackle one?"

"Pay your money, take your choice. Could be his sister's and the family's away visiting Aunt Mary. Could be his wife's just left him. What I'm thinking about right now, he did take some steps to get rid of the body." Palliser picked up the phone and called S.I.D. "That D.O.A. yesterday—you pick up anything else at the scene?"

"Didn't anybody call you? Well, we would have," said Horder. "It's busy down here. You'll get a report. Yeah, no latents anywhere on the body—you thought it'd been dropped there—but out back of that building we picked up a new-looking suitcase with some female clothes in it about the right size for the corpse, and an overnight bag ditto. We've just been over those, and there were some pretty good prints on the suitcase."

"Send the bags up if you're finished with them, will you? Thanks." Palliser relayed that to Glasser. "There you are. He dumped both her and the luggage there, maybe overlooking the plane case. The damn funny thing is, Henry, if he hadn't tried to set fire to the corpse she might not have been found until the powers that be finally came to demolish that building, which could be years."

"Fate," said Glasser. "That's so. Let's go have some lunch."

When Wanda brought Stephanie back she identified the suitcase immediately, and Sandra's overnight bag. Palliser took her prints to compare to those S.I.D. had collected from the suitcase, and they wasted an hour or so cruising around in the Rambler in the vicinity of that building on San Pedro. Stephanie was vague; it had been dark when Steve brought them to the house and dark when she ran away: she didn't recognize anything but the public library. So he brought her back, down to the Records office, and introduced her to Phil Landers.

"Mrs. Landers will give you some photographs to look at, Stephanie. If you recognize him, you tell her—or if you see any picture that might be him."

"Yes, sir, I'll look good. You're pretty sure it was him killed Sandra, aren't you?"

"Pretty sure." He left her to it, under Phil's eye.

"Why, yes, sir, I knew Dick Buford, very nice guy. Beg pardon? Oh, my name's Cutler. I couldn't believe it, I heard he got killed by a robber, right next door, and we never heard a thing!" Cutler was pleased at finding Landers and Grace on his doorstep, to talk about it. "Last person in the world you'd think—nice quiet fellow, him and his wife just devoted like they say till she passed on—" He rambled on, giving them nothing. He said he was a widower himself, that he'd been at the movies Tuesday night, when Buford had probably been killed.

At the house on the other side of Buford's they met a Mrs. Skinner who told them they'd just moved in, and if they'd realized it was the kind of neighborhood where murders happened they'd never have rented the house. She and Mr. Skinner had been at her sister's in Huntington Park on Tuesday night, got home late.

"All very helpful," said Grace, brushing his dapper mustache. "But the brother said he sometimes went up to a local bar for a few beers. Maybe he did that night."

"So what?" said Landers. "He was attacked at home."

"Well, we have to go through the motions."

Up on Virgil Street, in the two blocks each side, were three small bars. It wasn't quite noon, and only one was open. They went in and asked the lone bartender if he knew Buford. It was a little place, licensed for beer and wine only. He didn't react to the name or description. Pending the opening of the other two, they went to have some lunch, and Grace said over coffee, "A handful of nothing. It could've been any thug in L.A. picking a house at random to go after loot. The brother's supposed to look and see if anything's missing. Up in the air, like those damned funny rapes."

"I said we'd be in for another spate of the funny ones," agreed Landers. "And of course, if that kid is as young as those women say, he won't be in Records, that is to have prints and a mug-shot. Unless one of them happens to spot him on the street, there's no way to look. That is one for the books all right."

At one-thirty they went back to that block and tried Ben's Bar and Grill on the corner of Virgil. It was just open, no customers in. A fat bald fellow with a white apron round his middle was polishing the bar; it was just a small place, but looked clean and comfortable, with tables covered in red-checked cloths. "Do for you, gents?" asked the bartender genially.

Landers flashed the badge. "Is a Mr. Buford one of your regular customers here? Dick Buford?" He added a description. "Maybe he didn't come in often, just sometimes?"

The bartender's geniality vanished. "Oh," he said in a subdued tone, "yeah, that's so. Yeah, I knew that guy. I heard something happened to him—some guy down the street said he got killed. That's a shame, seemed like a nice guy. No, I didn't know him good, just a customer, not very often like you said."

"Was he here on Tuesday night?" asked Grace in his soft voice.

The bartender passed a fat hand across his mouth and said unwillingly, "I guess maybe he was. I guess it was

Tuesday. He never stayed long—two, three beers, and he'd go out."

"Did he get talking to anybody else here that night?"

"I don't remember. We were kind of busy, I didn't take any notice. He never stayed long, like I said, in and out. I don't remember what time it was."

"Remember any other regular customers here at the same time?" asked Landers.

"No. I couldn't tell you a thing. I'm not even sure now it was Tuesday," said the bartender. A couple of men came in and he turned his back on police.

"Well, do tell," said Grace outside. "That's a little funny, Tom. What's he feeling nervous about?"

"Just doesn't want to be mixed in—you know the citizens, Jase. This is a waste of time. The only way we'll find out what happened to Buford is if the lab picked up some good evidence at the scene."

Higgins had had some paperwork to clean up on a suicide from last week, and was the only one in when a call came from Traffic about a new body. It was a rooming house over on Beaudry, and the landlady had walked in to confiscate anything there until the rent was paid up, and found the tenant dead in bed. Higgins went to look at it.

Anywhere there was always the narco bit, the addicts and the pushers; these days something new had been added. Time was the heaviest traffic in the hard stuff was in heroin; a while back the H had started to be old hat, and the thing now was cocaine. It was just as lethal but it took a little longer to kill its victims. But the younger generation had added a refinement, and increasingly now they were picking up the kids half high on dope of one sort or another and half high on gin or vodka.

Higgins couldn't say exactly what might have taken off the fellow in the little bare rented room; the autopsy would tell them. But he didn't look over twenty-five, and there were needle-marks on both arms, not a dime in the place, a few old clothes, an empty vodka bottle beside the bed. No I.D. in the clothes, but the corpse was wearing a tattoo on one upper arm that said *Jacob Altmeyer* in a wreath of flowers. Higgins called up the morgue wagon and went back to Parker Center, down to Records.

"And how's Tom treating you these days?" he asked cute flaxen-haired Phil Landers as she came up. Phil smiled at him.

"So-so. I think his Italian blood's showing, he's getting stingy with a buck."

"God knows aren't we all these days."

"I understand," said Phil gravely, "that the baby's walking at last."

Higgins grinned unwillingly; he'd taken some kidding about that. Well, since he'd belatedly acquired a family, his lovely Mary and Bert Dwyer's kids Steve and Laura, and then their own Margaret Emily, he found he worried about them. And he'd never known any babies before, but by what everybody said they ought to start walking at about a year, and she hadn't, and he had worried. She'd been a year old in September. Mary said don't be silly, George, she's a big baby, she'll walk in her own good time. But he'd fussed about it, in case anything was wrong. And then suddenly, a couple of weeks ago, she'd got up and started walking just fine, and he'd been damned relieved. Probably bored everybody in the office about it.

"That's so," he said. "She's just fine. Have we got a Jacob Altmeyer on file anywhere?"

Phil said she'd look, and while she was gone Higgins thought about what Luis had said about the pretty boys.

When that had begun to show a pattern, not just the one-time thing, they had asked the computer about known threesomes at muggings, but that had come to nothing. Anyway, nothing said these three had been together very long. And even if Luis was right, and they didn't belong to this beat, there was no way to go looking for them.

Phil came back with a small package on Altmeyer. He had a rap-sheet of B. and E., possession, assault. Just another dopie, whatever he was on, supporting a habit which had finally removed him from his misery. There was an address for his mother in Glendale. Higgins went back to the office and got her on the phone to break the news.

After two days of threat, it had finally begun to rain again.

"Well, I don't know what to say," said the manager of the Globe Grill. "I suppose—my office isn't very big—you could use the dining room, we don't open that until four." He was a rather handsome sharp-faced man with friendly eyes and a quiet voice; his name was Rappaport. He eyed Mendoza, Conway and Galeano worriedly. "Police coming—you're a new bunch—but Marta's a good girl, and of course I've heard something about it. The damnedest thing—I don't understand it. We've got to cooperate with you, and I don't like to ask you, don't keep her—but it's working hours and we get kept busy here. If you want to go in the dining room, I'll get her."

Rappaport, and this whole place, was a little surprise. Galeano had taken it for granted, from Carey's report, that the blonde worked in a greasy spoon somewhere for peanuts. The Globe Grill, while down this side of Wilshire and not in the gourmet class of the better-known places out on La Cienega, was a quietly good restaurant. It was divided into a coffee shop on one side and a large dining room on the other, it was shining bright with cleanliness and polished chrome and sleek modern lighting, and was larger and busier than they had expected.

"Very nice," said Mendoza as they went past a red velvet curtain into a large dining hall with crystal chandeliers, red vinyl upholstery, a vaguely Mediterranean décor. The tables were octagonal, with low heavy chairs; he pulled out a chair, sat down and lit a cigarette.

"Maybe a little classier than we thought," agreed Conway. Galeano sat down too, and accepted a light from Conway.

The curtains parted. "Again, you want to ask questions? Oh, you are different police."

Carey's blonde was blonde only in the sense that she wasn't dark. Her thick hair was tawny russet to dark gold, obviously as nature made it, and she wasn't conventionally pretty; she had high wide cheekbones, a face slanted to a slender chin, a wide mouth, uptilted brows and grave dark eyes. She was only about five-three, and had a neatly rounded figure in her yellow and white uniform. She came farther into the room and all the men stood up formally.

"Mrs. Fleming? Lieutenant Mendoza—Detective Conway, Detective Galeano. Sit down, won't you?" Mendoza offered her a cigarette.

"Thank you, I do not smoke. You want to ask all the questions again?"

"Well, you see, Lieutenant Carey has passed the case on to my department." Mendoza was watching her. "Robbery-Homicide."

Her eyes didn't change expression; she looked down at her folded hands and said, "You think Edwin is dead. So do I." She had the faintest of accents; her speech betrayed her more by its formal grammar. "I thought that from the first."

"We've heard all the—mmh—circumstances from Carey," said Mendoza, emitting a long stream of smoke, "and you must admit it all looks very odd, doesn't it?"

"It is a mystery, yes," she said. "I have thought and thought, and I cannot decide what has happened." She was watching them too, looking from one to the other. "I am sure he has killed himself, but I do not understand how."

"Mmh, yes, it seems rather an impossibility." Mendoza's tone was only faintly sardonic. "When he was confined to a wheelchair, he couldn't even get downstairs by himself. And couldn't, of course, drive—though you have a car."

"We were going to sell it. A young man down the street wishes to buy it. It is too expensive to operate an auto now. No, he could not have driven."

"You told Carey your husband had threatened suicide?"

She said carefully, "He has been very—very despondent about life, since the baby died." Her mouth twisted a little. "He was fond of little Kätzchen. Before, he had been —a little optimistic, that perhaps in time the doctors could make him walk again. But lately, it was as if—he said, there was nothing, no reason to go on living, he was only a worry and a burden to me, and it was not right."

"And how did you feel about it? The same way?" asked Mendoza.

She looked surprised. "I? It was—a thing life had brought to us. How should I feel? I was sorry."

"Mmh, yes," said Mendoza. "You work long hours here? Walk to work and home again?"

"Yes. I am here mornings and evenings, six days a week." She looked at him impassively and then said, not raising her voice, "You do not believe me either. That other policeman, that Carey, he asked questions over and over again, who are our friends, do I have a special friend, perhaps a special man friend, what did I do that day, where did I go, were there any telephone calls—and the other girls here, Betty and Angela who work with me, he asked them questions about me. It is almost a little funny." But she was looking angry. "Do you all think I have murdered my husband? That is very funny indeed, how could I do that? Even if I were so wicked?"

"Did you?" asked Mendoza.

"Please do not be so foolish. I beg your pardon," she said tiredly. "I know the police always have to deal with criminals, wicked people, and perhaps you come to suspect everyone is so. You have to find out, ask questions, to know. But all I can do is tell you the truth. I do not know what has happened to Edwin."

Mendoza had stubbed out his cigarette, now lit another. "You came home that day, nearly two weeks ago— two weeks ago tomorrow—at about five o'clock? You got off here at two, and went shopping, you said. It was raining very heavily that day."

Her eyes fell before his. "Yes," she said. "Yes. I am— you forget—European, I am used to the rain."

For no reason Galeano's heart missed a beat. There was a curious purity of outline to her wide forehead, and that mass of tawny hair—she looked like a Saxon madonna. But this story—this impossible tale—and there, just one second, she had flinched over something.

"And found your husband gone? Missing from his wheelchair. Did you look for a suicide note?"

"Yes, yes, yes. I would have thought he would leave such a note, if he meant to kill himself. There was nothing. I looked all about the apartment building, I thought if he had jumped out a window—"

"But he couldn't have jumped," said Conway.

"No, no, a figure of speech. I have said all this before, it must be in reports. There was no one else in the house except the old man, Offerdahl. He was drunk, he could not say anything. I said, since we are living there, just a few times when I came home Edwin had been drinking, and it is this Offerdahl who has done it, brought him drink. I did not—"

"Did it make him less despondent?" asked Conway deadpan.

"No, it did not! It was very bad for him. All this, it is all I can tell you. When I had looked, I called the police and told them. Then this Carey came, and his men, and asked questions and looked at the apartment, and they did not believe me. Do you want to look at my apartment also?"

"Why, I think we would," said Mendoza cheerfully. "Thanks so much, Mrs. Fleming."

She stood up abruptly. "I will get you the key."

They watched her stalk past the curtain. "Now that is some blonde," said Conway. "Different type than I expected. And a very, very nice act. She's smart not to try to ham it up with my God what's happened to poor darling Edwin, I don't think she's that good an actress."

"You could be right," said Mendoza meditatively, and Galeano exploded at them.

"My good God in heaven, a child in arms could see that girl's as innocent and honest as—as a nun!" he said furiously. "Of course she's not acting, she wouldn't know how—I know what the story sounds like, but I'll be God-damned if I don't believe it, that girl is as transparently honest as—as—"

"*¡Qué hombre!*" said Mendoza, staring at him. "Don't tell me our confirmed bachelor has fallen for a suspect."

"You go to hell, of course I haven't fallen for her, if

you want to be vulgar," said Galeano. "But I'd think anybody could see—" He stopped as the curtains came apart
and she marched up to Mendoza, stiffly erect.

"Here is the key. You will know the address. I ask
only that you return it before I must go home, I have no
other. There are no secrets there, you may look as you
please."

"Thanks so much," said Mendoza. She marched out
again, her shoulders squared. "Saint Nicholas to the de-
fense of accused womanhood! We don't need Carey to
point out obvious facts. Who had a motive to be rid of
him?"

"You're only inferring that, as the cheap Goddamned
cynics you both are," said Galeano hotly. "For all we know,
she was still mad in love with him—"

"Ha-ha," said Conway. "And you've been on the
force how long?"

"Peace, *niños,*" said Mendoza. "Since the lady handed
over the key so obligingly, I'll believe her that far, there
aren't any secrets there. But I'd like to see the wheelchair,
and the general terrain. Come on."

He and Conway went on discussing it on the way over
there in the Ferrari, while Galeano sat in silence in the
little jump seat behind. For the first time he realized that
this job held a built-in hazard, just as she'd said: too many
cops, from too much experience, automatically expected
the lies, the hypocrisy, the guilt. Conway was a cynic from
the word go, but Galeano would have expected more in-
sight from the boss. That girl was so shiningly honest—and
when you thought what she'd been through— And then to
have all the cops come poking around suspecting her, *Dio,*
it was a wonder she'd been as polite as she had.

But just what, inquired the remnant of his common
sense, had happened to Edwin Fleming?

It was raining again. (Just why had she minded that question about her shopping trip?) The narrow old streets down from Wilshire were dispirited and drably gray in the drizzle. The six-family apartment, when they went into it, was silent as the grave. Everybody here out at work, except the bibulous Mr. Offerdahl. There was a tiny square lobby with a single row of locked mailboxes. They climbed uncarpeted stairs, steep and slanted old stairs—no, a man in a wheelchair couldn't have come down here, and if he had somehow crawled down, where had he gone from there?—to the second of three floors. There were two doors opposite each other in a short hall. Galeano remembered Mrs. Del Sardo across the hall, who had seen Fleming that morning as Marta said good-bye to him.

Mendoza fitted the key in the lock and opened the door.

It was a small, old, inconvenient apartment: what she could afford. But it was all as shiningly clean as the restaurant where she worked, furniture polished, stove and kitchen counter-top immaculate; that was a German girl for you, thought Galeano. There was the wheelchair, pushed to one side of the little living room, a steel and gray-green canvas affair. A few pieces of solid dark furniture, probably chosen with care at secondhand stores, possibly several pieces bought before his accident, when he was still earning and they were planning a home of their own. Just the one bedroom, sparsely furnished: a small square bathroom, a minimum of cosmetics in the medicine cabinet. She had wonderful skin, milk-white, evidently didn't use much on it.

"There is," said Mendoza, "only one little thing in my mind, boys." He looked out the rear window in the bedroom. "Yes, even as Carey said—who was to see anything there was to see?" This was a square building on a short lot. There was a single driveway to a row of six connected single garages across the back; and on the lot behind a building had recently been torn down. The old house across from the driveway was vacant, with a FOR RENT sign in front of it. "Just one thing," said Mendoza. "When did she have time?"

"Time for what?" said Conway. "She took care to have an alibi. We said—"

"Time to acquire the boyfriend. She's working eight hours a day, and Edwin must have taken up some more. On the other hand, there is Rappaport. Quite a handsome fellow. Right at the restaurant."

"Oh, for God's sake," said Galeano.

"And then again, a restaurant. Sometimes these things don't take all that long. Quite probably there are regular customers. And she could be out shopping on Sunday, on her afternoon break, without the neighbors noticing—there is that. But how in hell to locate him, if it isn't Rappaport—there won't be any letters—"

"Woolgathering!" said Galeano. "And you're supposed to be such a hot detective! If you can't see that that girl is honest as day—"

Mendoza shook his head at him. "You do surprise me, Nick. Let's see if Mr. Offerdahl is home." Carey had said he was down the hall; actually Offerdahl lived on the next floor. They climbed more steep stairs, knocked. There were fumbling sounds beyond the door; presently it opened and Offerdahl gazed blearily out at them.

He was the wreck of a once big man: still tall and broad-shouldered, but cadaverously thin, a few wisps of white hair on a round skull, his skin gray and flabby. He was not quite falling-down drunk, and a rich aroma of Scotch enfolded him.

"About Mr. Fleming," said Mendoza conversationally.

Offerdahl blinked. "You used to go see Mr. Fleming? The fellow in the wheelchair? Take him a little drink now and then to cheer him up?"

"Tha's right," said Offerdahl after a dragging moment. "Poor fella. Poor fella. Jus' young fella. Para-parapara-lyzed."

"Did you see him a week ago last Friday?"

"Oh, don't be silly," muttered Galeano. "He doesn't know March from December."

"Haven't you found the poor fella yet?" asked Offerdahl. "Strange. 'S very strange. Poor, poor fella." He leaned on the door jamb looking thoughtful, and suddenly added, "Good-bye," and shut the door.

"And what you think that was worth," said Galeano sourly, "I don't damn well know."

"Neither do I," said Mendoza. "Here—you take the key back to her, *amigo*. And for God's sake preserve your common sense."

Cunningly, Galeano waited until just before two o'clock to take the key back, and offered to drive Mrs. Fleming home through the rain. She thanked him formally, and emerged in a practical hooded gray coat over a subdued navy dress.

"I am sorry if I have offended your chief," she said in the car. "But it is so silly to ask the questions over and over."

Her profile was enchanting, with its little tilted nose and the wisp of tawny hair under the hood. Galeano nearly ran a light. "Well, we have certain routines to go through," he said. "Look, nobody suspects you, Mrs. Fleming. I mean, we can see you've had a bad time. What with everything."

She was silent. When he stopped in front of the apartment, went round and opened the door, she said, "Thank you—you are kind. I am sorry, your name—"

"Galeano. Nick Galeano."

"Mr. Galeano. Thank you." She ran into the apartment quickly and he stared after her, for a moment forgetting to put on his hat.

By five o'clock Stephanie had pored over a lot of mug-shots, and pointed out three though her responses were laced with doubt. "I mean, all of these look something like him. Not just exactly, but they could be."

Wanda shepherded her back to the Peacocks at the Holiday Inn. If this came to court, she'd be asked to identify X positively; as it was, Palliser and Glasser looked at the possibles she'd picked out with mixed feelings as well.

Steven Edward Smith: pedigree of B. and E. Richard Lamont: indecent exposure, assault with intent. Earl Rank: rape, B. and E.

"Two possibles, by their records," said Glasser. But the addresses were nowhere near downtown L.A., and they were fairly recent addresses; Lamont was just out of jail.

"People move around," said Palliser. "We can have a look at them, Henry."

FOUR

AFTER A COUPLE of quiet shifts, the night watch was busy. They had E. M. Shogart back, that stolid plodder who'd put in twenty years in the old Robbery office before it got merged with Homicide, and was still a little unreconciled to the change. He would be up for retirement next year if he wanted to take it, and probably would.

A rather bored Schenke was listening to Piggott talk about his tropical fish, an unlikely hobby which had seized him a while ago, when they got the first call, to a heist up on Seventh. Early, but time meant nothing to the punks. They both went out on it.

It was, expectably, a liquor store, and the owner had been there alone, just about to close. "I got this place up for sale," he told them, "and not before it's time. I been heisted four times the last nine months."

"Can you give us any description of him?" asked Schenke.

"Description? I could draw you a picture." The owner was a little fat man about sixty, named Wensink. "Talk about adding insult to injury, they not only walked off with the cash from the register, about a hundred and forty, they loaded up a station wagon with a thousand bucks' retail of my best stuff! There was three of them. One with the gun.

The one I saw best was that one. A guy maybe forty, medium-size, not much hair and he had one walleye. And what looked like a forty-five. All business, he was. The other two were younger, one with a mustache, the long hair."

"Well, that's a switch," said Schenke. "Taking the stock. A station wagon? You got a look at it?"

"I sure did," said Wensink. "They parked right in front, come in just at closing time. Anybody noticed them carrying stuff out, I suppose thought they were just customers. I didn't get a look at the license plate but it was a Ford nine-passenger wagon, white over brown, about five years old."

He thought the one with the gun might have touched the register, so they called out a man from S.I.D. to dust for prints. Wensink said he'd recognize a mug-shot and would come in tomorrow to look.

When they got back to the office, Shogart had gone out on another call; also a heist, he reported when he came in. An all-night movie-house on Fourth, and the girl in the ticket box was a nitwit, couldn't say anything except that he'd had a gun. "I wouldn't even take a bet on that. And God knows they deserve to lose some of their ill-gotten gains, it's a porno house."

"Amen to that," said Piggott, "but two wrongs, E. M.—" He was interrupted by the phone, and the Traffic man on the other end said he and his partner had just come across a body.

Schenke went out to look at it while Piggott typed up a report on the liquor-store heist. It didn't, said Schenke when he came back, look like any mysterious homicide to occupy the day watch: an old bum dead in a doorway over on Skid Row; but a report had to be written, an I.D. made if possible.

Piggott had just finished the first report and Schenke was swearing at the typewriter when the phone buzzed and Piggott picked it up. "Robbery-Homicide, Detective Piggott."

There was silence at the other end, and then a cautious male voice said, "You guys picked up Bobby Chard, you got him in your morgue. You read it he got took off by accident like. You better look again."

Piggott didn't ask who was calling. "Is that so? Why?"

"There was reasons." The phone clicked and was dead.

"Chard," said Piggott to himself. The one Traffic had thought was a hit-run. Well, maybe they'd better look three times instead of twice. Or it might be a mare's nest. He wrote a note for Higgins and left it on his desk.

On Friday morning, with Glasser off, Palliser roped Landers in to help out on the legwork on Sandra. The two likeliest suspects Stephanie had picked out of Records, on account of their pedigrees, were Richard Lamont and Earl Rank. Lamont's latest address was Burbank, Rank's Van Nuys, but as Palliser pointed out, people did move. They went looking.

Landers found Lamont after three tries. Lamont's sister in Burbank thought he might be staying with a pal in Hollywood; the pal said Dick was living with a woman in the Atwater section, and there Landers ran him to ground, in one side of an old duplex, watching TV.

Lamont fit Stephanie's description, down to the little goatee, but he told Landers earnestly he was real clean. Last time he'd been in, the judge had sent him to one of those head doctors, cured him from wanting to do funny things to girls, and he'd never do a thing like that again.

"So you can tell me where you were last Tuesday?" asked Landers.

Lamont thought. "All day, sir? Well, I was at my job all day, it's at McGill's garage out Vermont, Mr. McGill's teaching me all about engines and says I take to it good. I got to leave for the job pretty soon too, I don't go on till noon 'cause we're open tonight. I just come home—last Tuesday you mean, sir?—and Lilly Ann could say I was here, if that's good enough, sir. She's a real honest girl, never been in no trouble, we're fixin' to get married. She works at this upholstery place on Jefferson, you could ask and she'd say."

Landers went on to find Lilly Ann; there was no point in hauling Lamont in to lean on him heavier until they were a lot surer. Lilly Ann sounded positive, and had a clean record. This one was up in the air.

He came back to headquarters to find Palliser just bringing in a likelier suspect.

Earl Rank had the kind of record which made him likely, and he hadn't any alibi; he was living alone in a single room on Fourth, but Palliser had found him at his mother's place on a tip from a pal at the car-wash where he worked.

"A house down on Ceres," he told Landers. "Two-bedroom place, about what you'd expect, but it could tie in." Ceres Street was five blocks from San Pedro. "And his mother's just got back from visiting a married daughter in 'Frisco, how about that?"

"I like it," said Landers. "It ties in very neat. Let's see what he has to say about it."

They took him into an interrogation room and started asking questions. Rank was sullen and belligerent in turns, the usual attitude, and they didn't get much out of him.

"Don't you remember where you were last Tuesday, Rank?"

"Around. Just around." He was about thirty, a pale-skinned black with a wispy little goatee, a thin mustache, secretive eyes, a hard mouth. "I didn't do anything."

"We've got a witness who says maybe you did. You picked up any juvenile females to sweet-talk lately, Earl?" He'd done that at least once, by his record; the parents had reneged on letting her testify, and there'd been no prosecution.

"I never did no such thing. You can't prove I done nothing."

They couldn't. It might be interesting to hear what Stephanie would say about his mother's house on Ceres Street; but they'd have to show cause and get a court order even to take pictures, and she might not recognize pictures. It was just suggestive, no real evidence at all. "And you know, Tom," said Palliser, scratching his nose, "that girl was so scared, by her own admission, I wouldn't like to take her description of the man or the house as gospel truth. She couldn't be certain. You stop to think, she only saw the man three or four times—in a car at night, and at the house. She spent some time at the house, but we couldn't get much of a description—all she could say was, two bedrooms, no rugs, an old refrigerator, the TV was new. She also picked this other mug-shot, Steven Smith. He's got no sex counts, just B. and E., but I suppose there's always a first time. But I wouldn't bet on it."

"They do train us to be thorough," said Landers. "We'd better look for him too."

They let Rank go, at least temporarily, and went looking for Smith without any luck. He was off parole, he'd moved from the latest address in his file, and nobody admitted to knowing where he was. There were no relatives listed for him. He could be Stephanie's Harry, but he needn't be.

And Palliser said, "I tell you, Tom, I wouldn't rely

on that girl. If I felt surer she'd been sure about that description, I'd like Rank for it a lot. As it is, she picked out two other shots too. In a way, I think we'd be safer just going by the general description and looking at mug-shots ourselves."

"You do like to do it the hard way. You talked to her," said Landers with a shrug. "So where do we go from here?"

"We go call on Earl Rank's mother," said Palliser. "She may be a perfectly honest woman—nothing says she isn't, though she didn't like it much when I brought him in—and if Earl is the X on Sandra, possibly Mrs. Rank noticed something when she came home yesterday. Things missing from the refrigerator—or that nice little green-striped plane case he forgot to get rid of."

"Well, we can ask," said Landers. He didn't sound very hopeful.

Mendoza's insatiable curiosity had fastened on the strange case of Edwin Fleming. There wasn't much to be done, in the way of the usual routine, on the equally strange rape-assaults or the merely brutal pretty boys, but questions could be asked about Fleming. After a desultory glance at the night report, he went out to ask some; and he'd be covering ground Carey had already been over, but then Mendoza always preferred to ask the questions personally, and he flattered himself he'd get more out of those other girls than Carey had.

He started out at the Globe Grill, where he was resented because they were still busy with the late-breakfast trade. Rappaport wasn't there. He used the badge without compunction, aware that Marta Fleming was watching him with smouldering eyes. The first one he talked to was Betty

Loring, a black-haired buxom female of, he suspected, very medium intelligence.

"I don't know her very well, like I told the other cop. I mean, she's all business, she don't talk much to the rest of us. No, I don't mean she's unfriendly exactly, just quiet. What you mean, Mr. Rappaport? Oh, he's a real gentleman, he don't allow any funny business from customers. I worked some places" —she rolled her eyes— "but he's real strict. I don't get why you're asking about Marta, it's her husband something happened to, I guess. Cops! All this fuss over him going off."

The other one, Angela Norton, was older and brighter. She said curiously, "All you cops around, just on account of her husband. I don't know anything about it, she's a quiet one, but it seems funny. Didn't he just walk out?"

Mendoza told her about that, and she stared. "I didn't know that, about him being paralyzed. That's terrible. She never said a thing, and she's worked here nearly six months. But you don't mean you think she had anything to do with it? Honestly, she's—she wouldn't have—that other cop asking if she had boyfriends, that strikes me as silly, honestly —she's so serious, all business. If you want to know, it's my guess she's been awful homesick. That sounds silly too, but I think she is."

Mendoza was slightly taken aback. Cigarette halfway to his mouth, he said, "Why do you say that?"

"Oh, well—she's quiet like I said, but once we took a break together, and I forget what brought it up, somebody's birthday I think, but she got to talking about Germany, and her family—someplace they'd gone on a picnic for her sister's birthday, in the country, and she was all different, sort of gay and laughing hard. She'd never talked about her family to me before. I don't know what you're thinking about her, but honestly she's so straitlaced, I wouldn't think—"

"Cops don't tell what they think," said Mendoza absently. The other two waitresses here worked different hours, didn't know Marta as well even as these two had, and Carey hadn't got anything out of them. Mendoza didn't ask to talk to Marta; yesterday, with Carey's report in his mind, he'd thought he had read her, and been amused at Nick Galeano. Now he took the Ferrari up Vermont Avenue to the office of Dr. Sylvester Toussaint, and used the badge to pull rank again.

Dr. Toussaint, annoyed at having routine interrupted, answered questions briefly. "I hadn't seen Fleming in some time, there was nothing I could do for him after all. Nothing anybody could do, poor devil. He was referred to me by the specialist in therapy at the General—he hadn't had a regular physician, and it was just to keep an eye on him generally. Apart from the paralysis—the spine was almost completely severed—he seems to have made a good adjustment—ah, that is, physically. Quite a healthy specimen. Did I understand you to say he's *disappeared?* I don't see how—"

"Neither do we. He could manipulate the wheelchair by himself?"

"Oh, yes. The couple of times his wife brought him in here—as is often the case, he was developing extra strength in his arms. But," said the doctor, "but how on earth—"

"His wife thinks he's committed suicide. You said, the *couple* of times he was in. Not regularly? Not in how long?"

"I'd have to look at his file. Not for four or five months, I'd say. I told them there was nothing to be done, and there seemed to be some financial difficulty—there was no insurance. I told her there was no necessity for me to see him on a regular basis."

"You're an honest man, Doctor," said Mendoza dryly. "What did you think of her, by the way?"

Toussaint took off his glasses and polished them with his handkerchief. "Mrs. Fleming? She seems like a nice young woman—not much to say for herself. She took good care of him, I will say—he was clean and neat."

"Did he ever seem suicidal to you?"

Toussaint put his glasses back on. He was looking very interested now. "That's a difficult thing to say about anybody, Lieutenant. But the last time I saw him—well, he felt resentful, which I suppose we can both understand. A man his age, a hopeless invalid. He said to me, he could live to be eighty, and it wasn't fair to his wife. He'd be better off to cut his throat and save everybody the trouble, he said."

Mendoza cocked his head at him. "He said it just like that—cut his throat? I see. *Interesante.*"

"But evidently he didn't," said the doctor. "How could he have disappeared?"

Mendoza got up and yanked down his cuffs. "Simpler if he had cut his throat. And if he thought of suicide in those terms, and really wanted to—but if I've learned one thing at this job, Doctor, it's that you never can tell what people will do. As I suppose you have, too. Thanks so much." He left the doctor looking very curious, and ambled slowly back downtown in traffic a little heavier than usual, in the gray mist.

Before he got off the freeway it began to rain again in a hesitant way, short of storm but getting everything very wet. The little side street down from Wilshire was empty, only an occasional car parked along the one side where parking was legal. He was on the wrong side, and had to back and fill around four times to turn the Ferrari's length. He walked across the street and down the drive of the apartment house. All the garages but one were open and empty; the exception was the one at the left end, and he went around to peer into the little window. Inside was a middle-aged tan Dodge sedan, and by Carey's report that would be the car owned by Edwin Fleming, the car too expensive to run, which they'd been going to sell. There'd be some red tape to that now, without his signature.

He wondered suddenly if she had a driver's license. How had she got him to the doctor's office?

He went back up the drive and into the building. It was as silent as it had been yesterday, everybody out at work. Anything could have gone on here, damn it, and nobody been the wiser. The Archangel Gabriel could have swooped down and carried Fleming off, with no witnesses. More realistically, how easy it would have been for the boyfriend—Rappaport or somebody else—to have walked in, got into the apartment by the simple expedient of ringing the bell, and knocked Fleming out.

"¿De veras?" said Mendoza to himself. But why in hell's name take him away? If that had been the general plan, to fake a suicide, easy enough to slash Edwin's throat, cut his wrists, leave the knife there with his prints on it, and walk quietly off. There was a good solid suicide, with a reasonable motive behind it, and likely nobody would have asked questions.

Mendoza was annoyed. Untidiness always annoyed him, and the strange case of Edwin Fleming was very untidy.

He climbed another flight of stairs and paused outside the right-hand door. Beyond it Mr. Offerdahl was feeling happy. Filtered through whiskey, the sound of singing emerged into the hall; Mr. Offerdahl was forever blowing bubbles.

The new call went down just after Mendoza left the office, and Hackett and Higgins went out to look at it. Over the years, they had gone together to look at a number of things like it, not that that reconciled them to the necessity; but in the last couple of years there seemed to be more and more such things to go and look at.

"Mr. Weinstein found her and called in," said the uniformed man waiting by the squad car. "It's a mess. He's got the pawnshop next door, knew her. Says her name's Mrs. Ruth Faber. I guess it must have happened last night."

They went in to look. This was a side street off Olympic, still downtown but the kind of half-and-half neighborhood old sections of big cities sprout. There was an access alley between two rows of old two-story buildings here, the first floors business places, old apartments above. This place was a little grocery store. There was a sign over the door that had been there a long time, FABER'S MARKET. Just one big room inside, a small refrigerator case, three walls of shelves with cans and packages, a wooden counter with an old-fashioned cash register, a Coke machine. In the middle of the uncarpeted pine floor lay the body of an old lady, horridly dead. There was blood all around and on her, and they couldn't tell what she'd looked like in life because her face had been beaten or kicked in. She was a thin old lady, wearing a cotton housedress, and one black felt slipper had fallen off, lay on a pair of smashed steel spectacles five feet from the body.

"What a mess," said Higgins. "Stop where you are, Art, or the lab boys'll chew you out. They'll have a field day here." There wasn't anything they could do until the lab men had processed the place for physical evidence, so they called S.I.D. and went to talk to Weinstein, who was waiting at the curb with the Traffic man.

"Yi," he said, "they hire you plainclothes fellows by the yard?" He looked at the two big men with sorrowful interest. He was a squat, square man with a dark good-humored ugly face and very bright black eyes. "This is just a terrible thing. The things that go on nowadays— You read about it, it don't touch you till it happens to somebody you know. What gets me, being in business, it used to be the places got held up, robbed, were places where any-body'd know there'd be loot—jewelry stores, banks, mil-lionaires' houses—you know? These days, any place. Half these hoods are high on something, don't know what the hell they're doing."

"What can you tell us about this, Mr. Weinstein?" asked Hackett. "You knew her?"

"Nothing much I can tell. That poor old lady, Mrs. Faber, I knew her since I been in business here, that's thirty years. She and her husband had that little market there maybe forty years, longer. She always ran it, and it was ridiculous she still did. I told her so. She made nothing on it, if she cleared fifty a month that'd be about it, people have cars now, go to the supermarkets. She didn't need to, she had her husband's pension from the railroad—he's been gone ten, twelve years. You ask me, it was habit—she didn't know how to stop. She lived in the apartment upstairs, and she must've been eighty if she was a day. The place was always open when I came to open up mornings, and I'd look in, say good morning. You could say I kind of kept an eye on her—old like she was, she could have a stroke, heart attack, and she hadn't any family at all. So, today"—he gestured eloquently—"I look in, there she is. My God. The poor old soul, these thugs around. At least, for what it's worth, they didn't get much, I hope."

"How's that?" asked Higgins.

"Yi, these old ladies," said Weinstein. "She was old-fashioned, kept her business to herself, which is O.K., but she'd got to know me all this time, that I'm O.K. too, and about six months ago she gives me nearly a heart attack myself. I go in to get a Coke. It was just after that big bank job uptown, and I mentioned it, and she says she never put any trust in banks, keeps her money where she can lay her hands on it. I had a fit, I talked to her like a brother. She was a close old lady, didn't spend much on herself, and God knows what she mighta had there, saved up fifty years, in a drawer or a closet shelf or somewhere. She finally listened to me and got a lock-box at the bank, I know that, she told me about it."

"You don't say," said Hackett, exchanging a glance with Higgins. The mobile lab truck slid to the curb behind the squad car. "Well, we'll ask you to make a statement later, Mr. Weinstein."

"Whatever I can do, gents." He turned away to the little pawnshop across the alley from the market.

"Maybe the word hadn't got round," said Higgins, watching Marx and Horder unload equipment from the truck.

"Or maybe," said Hackett, "it was just what the man said—a hood high on something who didn't know what he was doing. Bears the general resemblance to our pretty boys, only they've been grabbing them off the street. And this kind of violence is not so unusual now." It was to be hoped the hood had left some clues behind for the lab.

Galeano was just as glad it was Rich Conway's day off. He expected Rich wouldn't know when to stop kidding him about that blonde. It was like a lot of things in life, he thought: it came back to people, not facts. Maybe people versus facts. Damn it, he thought, when you heard a story like that, you said fishy, you said the gall, but meeting that girl—

As he rode up in the elevator, it came to him more clearly just why she'd made an impression on him, and it was a funny word to use: dignity. And maybe that was why Carey and Conway and, for God's sake, Mendoza, had reacted the way they had. If she'd gone all to pieces, nobody would have thought twice about it, just about the mystery . . . though, of course, anything happened to a husband you automatically looked at the wife, and vice versa . . . but, maybe on account of her different upbringing or something, Marta had that dignity, didn't go parading her feelings in public, and the cynics naturally thought she hadn't any.

Damn it, I'll believe her, thought Galeano. That it happened just that way: she'd come home and he was gone. But how and where? And why? The thing didn't make any sense.

Say he had been murdered by somebody else, there was no earthly reason to conceal the body, was there? But ruminating on it, Galeano had come up with a couple of ideas which might open the case wider. Carey had been thinking just about Marta, and the hypothetical boyfriend; but what about Edwin? There he was all day in his wheelchair, nothing to do. Maybe he listened to the radio, watched TV some, but not all day. They'd only moved to that place a couple of months ago. It could be that he'd spent some time on the phone, talking to old friends where they used to live in Hollywood; they had had friends there. Carey hadn't located all of them to talk to. It could be, thought Galeano vaguely, that somebody who hadn't heard about this could give them some ideas about Edwin. Anyway, they ought to chase down everybody who knew the Flemings.

Mendoza had gone out somewhere, and Lake was hunched over one of his eternal books about dieting. Galeano slid into Mendoza's office and found the manila envelope with Carey's notes, rummaged through it and took down addresses. People named Frost, Cadby, Prescott, Deal, up in Hollywood: Cahuenga Boulevard, Berendo, Las Palmas.

He drew a blank at the Cahuenga Boulevard apartment; a neighbor just going out told him that Mr. and Mrs. Cadby both worked. He drove down to Berendo. This was the place the Flemings had been living before his accident: one of the old Hollywood streets getting refurbished these days, old houses torn down to make way for new apartments. It was a new, brightly painted two-story building with balconies on the upper floor units, a small blue pool in a side yard, patio tables. The Prescotts lived upstairs at the back; he rang the bell and waited.

The girl who opened the door was a slim leggy brunette in slacks and turtleneck sweater. "Yes?" She looked at the badge in his hand with surprise.

He said economically he'd like to ask a few questions about the Flemings—people who used to live here. "You knew them?"

"Why, yes. What's the matter, they're not in any trouble, are they? Pat, it's a cop about Marta and Ed. This is Mrs. Frost, er—"

"Galeano."

"Mr. Galeano. I'm Marion Prescott. Pat knew them too. But what *is* the matter? What do you want to know?"

The other girl was smaller, blonde, with a rather scraggly figure. Galeano told them that Fleming was missing and enquiries were being made. "Missing!" said Marion Prescott. "How could he be missing? He couldn't just walk away, a man in a wheelchair. That poor man! It made us all feel guilty, for—"

"For what?" asked Galeano as she stopped.

"Oh, heavens, you'd better come in," she said. "It's cold with the door open. Pat and I were just having some coffee, would you like some? I'll get you a cup, sit down."

"I can't get *over* it," said Pat Frost with avid interest. "You mean he's just disappeared? How funny. It's not as if he had any imagination."

"How do you mean?" asked Galeano.

"Oh, you know, like all those stories with ingenious plots, people vanishing and then turning out to be the mail carrier," she said vaguely. Mrs. Prescott came back and handed Galeano a cup of coffee.

"There's cream and sugar on the coffee table. Heavens, I suppose we'd better tell you whatever you want to know. Not that we knew them well, and we couldn't tell you anything about them since they moved away. It was just, we all lived here, and none of us was working—the wives, I mean—we'd have morning coffee and so on. Marta—she's not an easy person to know, would you say, Pat?"

"What did you mean about feeling guilty, Mrs. Prescott?"

"Oh—" She flushed. "You'll think we're a lot of snobs. Ed's a nice fellow, but, well, let's face it, he hasn't much education, many interests outside baseball and the corniest shows on TV. I don't mean the rest of us are intellectuals, for heaven's sake, but my husband's a broker and Pat's is a therapist at the Cedars, and the few times we all got together for a potluck supper by the pool, you could see Ed was out of his depth, he just didn't have anything to talk about to the men. Now Marta's very well educated, in that very correct German way, I'd say, and I could see she was embarrassed for him. And then when he had that accident, and was paralyzed—"

"Didn't he have some kind of pension or disability pay or something?" asked Pat Frost; her nose twitched with curiosity just the way Mendoza's did, Galeano noticed. "We wondered, but she never said a word, and then when they moved—he must have had, hadn't he? I mean, these days everybody—I know there was a fuss, the man he was working for claimed it was Ed's own fault, but we did hear he had to pay for the hospital—"

Marta not parading her troubles in public, that just confirmed his convictions. "I'm afraid I couldn't say about that. Have any of you been in touch with Fleming since they moved?"

"Heavens, no," said Marion Prescott. "It was just proximity, you could say. We hadn't much in common. As I say, Marta's difficult to know. Maybe the foreign upbringing, but she's so formal—well, I'll say one thing, I think she was homesick, she missed her family, she was always writing to them. I don't think she'd made any close friends here, I gather they'd moved around a good deal since Ed was out of the service."

"And I'll tell you something else," said Pat Frost, her eyes bright with interest in gossip. "And that is, Marta wasn't in love with Ed and never had been. I got the idea she just married him to get here and have more money, a better life. Well, she got disappointed there, Ed ending up in a wheelchair." She laughed.

Galeano looked at her with dislike, and decided the laugh was malicious. "You can't say that for certain, Mrs. Frost."

"Well, girls do know girls, don't we, Marion?"

"She was awfully broken up about the baby," said

Marion hastily. "A darling little girl, she was named Elisa for Marta's sister."

"Have either of you seen her since they moved? Has she contacted either of you?" And why would she, these two lightminded women, what had they in common? "Neither of your husbands been in touch with Fleming?"

"I told you, there'd be no reason," said Marion. "We were sorry—when that happened to him—but that's all there was to it. I don't even know where they moved."

"I see," said Galeano, and stood up.

"Do the police think Marta had something to do with Ed's disappearing?" Pat Frost's eyes were uncomfortably sharp. "He is—was—a lot of care, I suppose. My goodness, Marion! If she did something—my goodness! But I wouldn't be surprised, is all I can say."

"That's slander, Mrs. Frost," said Galeano mildly.

"Don't tell me Marta's corrupted our cops, Mr. Galeano," she said sweetly.

Marion Prescott said, "Yes, your Jack did rather fall for her, didn't he, dear? Until you hauled him back into line."

Galeano escaped.

He'd have to put that in a report, and what it sounded like—Conway and Mendoza would pounce on that Jack Frost, God, what a name, for the boyfriend. There was nothing in it, couldn't be anything in it: lots of men would be attracted to Marta. And Carey had talked to the Cadbys, said they hadn't had any contact recently. Which was exactly what they would say if there was any reason not to admit it.

Yielding to impulse, Galeano stopped at the Globe Grill for an early lunch. The place was crowded and another girl waited on him, but he could see Marta across

the coffee shop, neat in her uniform. Yes, a lot of men—
more money, a better life. He didn't know what place she
came from. There were still a lot of places in Europe, off
the beaten track, where people still thought all Americans
were millionaires. *She got disappointed there.* So there she
was, with a husband less well educated, likely not much in
common (after the baby died), and then a permanent
invalid.

She happened to turn and catch his eye on her just
then, and a slight flush showed on her cheekbones, her
wide mouth tightened.

Cops keeping an eye on her, thought Galeano. Suspecting her.

But he retained a wide streak of peasant common
sense, and as he picked up his bill, it suddenly said to him,
What did she gain by it? Which was a question.

Read it the obvious way, that the hypothetical boyfriend was to get rid of Edwin—fake a suicide, the easiest
thing. Galeano couldn't imagine any circumstances in
which that would have gone so wrong as to necessitate
taking the body away. But even if it somehow had, and
there was no blood, nothing suspicious in the apartment,
they'd have got together to make up a tale. Ed was in the
hospital for more tests; he was sick in bed and couldn't be
seen. There was just no reason at all for her to tell the
LAPD that very funny story—unless it was true.

Damn it, thought Galeano, that is an honest girl.

When he got back to the office, ready to argue the
case with Mendoza, he found Hackett and Higgins just
sitting, Hackett reading a report just typed, and Grace on
the phone. Higgins told him about the new one. They were
hoping the lab could give them a lead. It had already given
them a lead on one of the heists last night, at the liquor
store: the boys had picked up a dandy set of latents from

the cash register, being run through to see if they were in Records. If not LAPD's, maybe somebody's: NCIC or the FBI would tell them.

Grace put the phone down and said, "That's funny."

"What?" asked Higgins.

"That bartender," said Grace. "Who was nervous. When Tom and I asked him about Buford coming in that night. A funny little thing, and funny little things make me nervous. I just thought I'd find out about him. And—"

"Goddamn!" said Higgins suddenly. "Talking about funny little things just reminded me. Matt had an anonymous call—somebody said that Robert Chard thing was a deliberate kill. Probably means damn all."

"Anyway," said Grace, brushing his mustache back and forth, "that bartender—his name's Reinke, Charles Reinke—owns that place, holds the liquor license, which in this state says he's very clean and respectable. Which is also funny."

"The boss here?" asked Galeano.

"I don't know where he is," said Hackett.

Mendoza came in briskly, announced that it was still raining, and went into his office. Galeano followed him and without preamble gave him the gist of what he'd turned up. "If it means anything," he added. "Which I'm not convinced it does. For one thing, I just don't see what it gained her to tell that tale. If there'd been collusion to kill him and something went wrong, why in hell hide the body? And even so, why should she—"

"De acuerdo," said Mendoza. "I got there too, Nick. But I can imagine circumstances where—mmh—she couldn't very well have done anything else. Jack Frost. ¡Porvida! But we'd better talk to him. Just in case." He opened the top drawer of the desk and brought out the inevitable pack of cards, stacked it neatly on the blotter, got out a cigarette and operated the flame-thrower. "That's a very curious thing. Homesick, she said."

"Oh, Luis," said Higgins, poking his head in, "I forgot to tell you about this anonymous call on that Chard. And S.I.D. just called, they made those prints off that heist last night, he was in our records, Roy Titus. Art and I are just going out to have a look for him. They picked up some latents from that new job, the old lady, but they aren't processed yet."

"Bueno." Mendoza took the deck in his long, strong hands and began to shuffle it. "Good hunting." He squared the deck and cut it precisely to show the ace of diamonds.

"Oh, yes, I've seen you do that before," said Higgins, and went out. Mendoza shuffled, squared the deck and cut it to the ace of spades; shuffled and cut the ace of hearts.

"Plotting," he said absently to Galeano, "can be complicated. Most of what we see isn't plotted. Anything but."

"I see what you mean," said Galeano. Mendoza cut the deck, contemplated the ace of clubs, and the phone buzzed. He picked it up.

Loud enough for Galeano to hear, it sneezed at him. "Hello, Luis."

"God bless you, Saul. What do you want?"

"We've got a very pretty little homicide for you," said Lieutenant Goldberg of Narcotics, and blew his nose. "You want to come look at it? Damn these allergies. Pat and I are both here, it's a very classy apartment on Wilshire. Do come and see, Luis, we've got something interesting to show you."

"¡Condenación!" said Mendoza resignedly. "What's the address?"

FIVE

GALEANO AND GRACE went along to see what it was. The address was one of the new high-rise buildings out on Wilshire; Galeano could never get used to calling them condominiums when they were just glorified apartments. There was a black and white at the curb; Mendoza slid the Ferrari into a red zone and they got out.

"Where's Goldberg?" he asked the uniformed man by the squad car.

"Fourth floor, this side, sir. And thanks for the excuse to get out of there. I'm waiting for the men from the zoo, tell him I'll send 'em right up."

"The zoo?" said Grace. But Mendoza was already at the door.

The elevator took its time, eventually decanted them on the fourth floor. Down a plushly carpeted hall they spotted another navy uniform and made for it. "Homicide," said Mendoza. "This is it?"

"Oh, brother, you said it," said the Traffic man. "I'd rather have a riot to handle any day, at least with people you sometimes know where you are. Lieutenant Goldberg said you're to go straight in." He opened the door behind him gingerly, a crack, peered in, and opened it wider for them.

It was class, all right: rich deep carpeting, hotel-size furniture, damask draperies, in a big rectangular living room with a wall of window offering a view of the city. Lying face down under the window was a dead man, blood around him on the chaste carpeting. He was a chesty middle-aged man in a natty gray suit. Lieutenant Saul Goldberg, thin and dark and looking less morose than usual, was standing at one end of the long velvet-upholstered sofa, and at the other end stood Captain Patrick Callaghan also of Narcotics, incredibly bigger than Hackett and redder-haired than Alison. He looked rather pale, and his eyes were glued to the closed door opposite.

"Well, hello, Luis," said Goldberg. There was another man sitting on the couch, a rather fat middle-aged man in very expensive-looking sports clothes, an exquisite shade of fawn. He had jumped nervously when the door opened. There was a large, long wooden packing crate in the middle of the room with a lot of straw in it.

"Don't let it out!" said the man on the couch.

"We won't let it out," said Goldberg.

"What in hell goes on here?" asked Mendoza.

"This is Mr. Enoch Hoyt. A longtime narco dealer, just a couple of years ago graduated to the big time of smuggling. That," said Goldberg, nodding at the dead man, "was his partner, Mr. Delmar Underwood."

"I didn't mean to shoot him," said Hoyt aggrievedly. "I told you it was an accident. Anybody might have— Are you sure that door's shut, for God's sake?"

"So what happened?" asked Mendoza.

Goldberg blew his nose deliberately. "We got a hot tip that there was a big shipment of stuff coming in from Central America—coke mostly, some H. We'd known all about Mr. Hoyt and Mr. Underwood for some time, we were just waiting to get the goods on them. The ingenuity

that goes into the criminal trades—like with the con-
men, if they used that much genius in legitimate channels
they'd all be millionaires—"

"This pair don't seem to have done too badly," said
Mendoza, looking around.

"We got on to San Diego, but those boys were just
too late to catch it at the border, they'd already signed
for it and got through Customs. Mr. Hoyt had some pretty
forged papers identifying him as an assistant curator at
the Los Angeles Zoo."

"I can hear the damn thing in there, Saul," said
Callaghan. He hadn't taken his eyes from the door.

"I don't suppose you keep up with the latest dodges
for smuggling in the dream powder, Luis. This is one of
the newest. You see, snakes don't eat very often. The big
ones. So you stuff your shipment of coke or H or whatever
in a big plastic bag, and you get the snake to swallow
it with the rest of its once-a-month dinner, and then
you shut it up in a crate and address it to the Chief
Herpetologist, L. A. Zoo, and when it gets to Customs at
the Mexican border somebody like Mr. Hoyt—"

"I will be damned," said Mendoza.

"What kind of snake?" asked Galeano nervously.

"Well, I only got a very brief look at it," said Goldberg, "before I slammed the door, but the manifest says
it's a boa constrictor."

"I said it was just plain nuts!" said Hoyt plaintively.
"I didn't want nothing to do with it—I know it's the
latest gimmick, going smooth as damn-it here and New
York and Miami, and our latest consignment got picked
off by the Mexico City cops, damn it, and Del said to try
it, we had a contact in Guadalajara—but I never liked the
idea from the start—"

"Supposedly," said Callaghan, his eyes on the door,

"the snake is dormant, and when they've got it through Customs they just knock it on the head, slit it open and recover the—"

"Dormant!" said Hoyt wildly. "Say, listen, that's what Del said, he knew some guys been doing it for months, no trouble at all, but— Dormant? When he pried up the nails on that damn box, that Goddamned snake came out like a bolt of lightning, about fifty feet of it, and my God, I never meant to shoot *Del,* but I'd got my gun out just in case and the damned thing was all over the floor, I just—"

Something heavy landed against the closed door with a thud, and Callaghan flinched.

"It was at this interesting juncture," said Goldberg, "that Pat and I arrived, armed with a search warrant—we hoped they hadn't had time to get rid of the shipment to their dealers—and I'd just knocked on the door when the gun went off, so we came charging in."

"Ugh!" said Callaghan.

"To find Mr. Hoyt screaming and waving a gun around, and the, er, party of the first part disappearing into the bedroom. So I shut the door. I'm not a great pet lover myself. You can take Hoyt away and book him anytime. We're waiting for some men from the zoo to corral the boa. We'll ask if there's any way to make it disgorge the goods without killing it—it'd be a shame, poor thing, after it's performed such a good deed in getting Delmar put away."

"Yes, please, I'd like to get booked in right away," said Hoyt, getting up anxiously.

"The damn thing's working on the door," said Callaghan. "Where the hell are those herpetologists?"

Mendoza was laughing. "The things we run into— we'll take him off your hands, boys. Send me chapter and verse for the report. And do have fun with the snake charmers."

"Ugh!" said Callaghan. "I don't think I'm a coward, but I don't like snakes. I just don't like 'em."

Galeano was just as relieved to be out of that place, headed for the Alameda jail with Hoyt in a squad car. He didn't like snakes either. No way.

Sometimes, said Hackett to Higgins, this damn job was so monotonous and so easy that you might as well be on an assembly line screwing in bolt forty-six. The automatic routine turned up the answer like a coin bringing you the candy bar out of the machine. And it made you feel tired, dealing with the stupid, stupid punks.

This particular punk, who was old enough to know better, had left a nice set of prints on that cash register last night, and the lab boys had had no trouble at all in locating them in LAPD records and marking him as Roy Titus, who had a long record of such stupidities behind him. He was forty-five now and had a record going back to age twelve, mostly armed robbery, B. and E., a couple of muggings and two burglaries. He'd served some time, not as much as he should have; and at the moment he was still on parole, which meant that his current address was on file.

It wasn't even very far away from headquarters, on Budlong Avenue. Hackett and Higgins drove up there, in Higgins' car instead of the scarlet Barracuda in case they found him. It was an old apartment building, and before they parked they spotted Titus talking to a man in the driveway, so they went up to him and started to inform him of his rights. The other man looked surprised and asked what was going on.

"Who are you, anyway? What right you got to butt

in on a private deal? You want a piece of the action, you wait your turn!"

"What deal?" asked Hackett.

"Oh, hell," said Titus. "How'd you know I pulled anything?"

He had the haul from the liquor store neatly stacked in his garage; the other fellow lived down the block and on being offered a case of good whiskey at a quarter the retail price, wasn't about to ask questions. He was annoyed to miss out on the deal.

At this end of a day, Hackett and Higgins were not disposed to waste time questioning Titus about the two pals who'd pulled the job with him. They stashed him in jail; the warrant would be through presently, and they'd ask him about his pals tomorrow.

Hackett called Mr. Wensink and told him most of the liquor had been recovered, but it would be impounded as evidence; he'd get it back eventually.

"Maybe not me," said Wensink. "I think I got a buyer for this place, and I'm getting out. I'm getting too old to worry about heisters all the time I'm open for business. I'm going to retire and move to the country somewhere."

Higgins went home, and after kissing Mary and going in to see Margaret Emily peacefully asleep in her crib, went back to the garage to call Steve Dwyer in to dinner. "He's been out in that darkroom ever since he got home from school, and I know he's got homework," said Mary.

"I don't know why in hell," Higgins said to Steve, "you're set on being a cop. Most boring job there is a lot of the time."

"Not on the lab end," said Steve. "Gee, isn't the place peaceful without Laura at the piano all the time!" Laura had permission to stay overnight with a girl friend. But dinner wasn't exactly restful, the Scottie Brucie bouncing under their feet, and Steve anxious to get back to his photographic experiments.

"Just until nine o'clock," said Mary firmly. "I'll call you."

"Oh, Mother! It's Friday night!"

"Well, nine-thirty."

"He may invent a new camera or something and make us millionaires," said Higgins. "I don't know why I didn't go in for the lab end. No brains, I guess. Sometimes I think it rubs off on us, the stupid people we have to deal with."

"Now, George," said Mary.

Mendoza went home, still thinking about that snake, and Mrs. MacTaggart greeted him at the door with relief. "If you'd take them off my hands while I get at the dinner, then—Alison's better, she's had a good long nap, but I want to get that soufflé in."

"Daddy, come on—" Johnny pulling his arm urgently —"I want to show you what we learned in school today—" "Listen to me first, Daddy, I can say a new poem—" Terry clinging to the other arm. The twins had been in nursery school for three months and on the whole the effect was good; they were speaking English—most of the time, at least. Mendoza kept them occupied in the living room until Alison came in, looking more like her usual self, when they erupted at her.

"*Mamacita*, you listen to my new poem—" "It's a silly poem, Mama, I can do the Pledge of 'Legiance real good now—"

"The darlings," said Alison fondly when Mairí had taken them off to their baths. "Yes, I'm better—knock wood. And I've got something to show you, Luis. House plans. Well, you can't deny it, this will be too small when the baby comes. And we ought to have more yard. Later on we might want a pool—"

"*¡Despacia!*" said Mendoza. "I can see you're feeling better, plotting to spend more money."

There was fish for dinner, and the cats sat on their feet under the table reminding them that cats liked fish too. Cedric, who didn't, went away in disgust and brought in a dead bird from the backyard.

On Saturday morning Mendoza had just come in and said good morning to Sergeant Farrell, who sat in for Lake on days off, when an agitated voice said, "Oh, Sergeant Hackett!" Mendoza turned to see Hackett behind him. "I had to come, I got to make you listen—I tell you, they're gonna kill that lady! Honest to God they are! They were talkin' about it again, I heard 'em!"

Hackett looked down at Mr. Yeager and wondered if the man was slightly nuts. Hearing voices. "Now, look, Mr. Yeager—"

"No, you gotta listen to me, you gotta do something! They're goin' to murder her!" Yeager yanked at his sleeve in excitement. "I heard 'em say so!"

"Where were you this time?" asked Hackett. "Fixing the faucet in the kitchen? I'm sorry, Mr. Yeager, but I just can't believe—"

"You gotta listen to me!" Yeager looked ready to cry. "I tell you, I heard 'em say so!"

"How?"

Yeager took a step back. "Well, I did. I did so. I— the door was open, and him and his girl friend—"

Hackett had met his share of the nuts, and Yeager was

not unlike some he'd met, the ones with fixed ideas, mild delusions. He wasn't wasting time on figuring out this one, and caught Farrell's eye. He said gently, "Now look, Mr. Yeager, I looked at this and there's nothing to it. Suppose you go on home and stop worrying about it." He brushed past as Farrell took Yeager's arm and started ushering him out. Grace and Conway had just come in.

"What's that about?" asked Mendoza.

"Nothing," said Hackett. "Makes you wonder about Freud. He said he didn't like these people, and I suppose a confirmed Freudian would say he just wants to get them in trouble. These Lamperts. I went and looked around a little, but there's nothing to it. Well, one like that Roy Titus might go discussing a projected murder with the door open, but this Lampert doesn't seem to be working regular but seems to be on perfectly good terms with his mother— looks like a weak sister to me. I just can't see—I hope Yeager isn't going to be a nuisance."

Mendoza went on into his office. Hackett collected Higgins when he came in and they went up to the jail to follow up on Titus. Palliser roped Conway in with Landers to get back at the legwork on Sandra. Galeano, Grace and Glasser were still there when Scarne came in with some S.I.D. reports, and the autopsies came up from Bainbridge's office at the same time.

"So let's see what we've got, boys," said Mendoza. He glanced over the autopsies first. "There you are, the girl was raped and strangled. Short and sweet. Not, obviously, where she was found." He handed the report to Palliser, who'd just been leaving when Scarne came in. "What did the lab get on her clothes and so on? ¡Condenación! Those prints on the suitcase belong to Stephanie Peacock. Very helpful. And that is that. Nada absoluta-

mente. . . . Buford. Well, that gives us a little, not much. He died of a skull fracture. The lab found blood and hair on the leg of a chair in the house, hair his, blood his type. Inference, there was a scuffle with somebody and he was knocked down and cracked his skull."

"The door wasn't forced," said Grace. "He must have let the somebody in."

"So it was somebody he knew."

"Somebody he'd just had a run-in with at that bar, and the bartender knew it, but why the hell shouldn't he tell us? Unless—" Grace paused, looking thoughtful. "Well, I'd like to know more about him, that's all."

"Not even any surprises about the time of death. Both Tuesday night. Sandra between seven and ten, Buford between ten and midnight." Mendoza slapped the reports down. "Are you sure enough about that Rank to ask for a search warrant on the house, John?"

"No," said Palliser. "It's fifty-fifty. He could be X, but we'd never pin it down. If that plane case was there, it isn't now. But I get the impression—just the impression—that his mother's an honest woman, and she says he doesn't have a key to the house. It's a double deadbolt. We can't really rely on Stephanie's identification, anyway. I think we do it from scratch, look at men with the right records and weed 'em out by the general description. The right one might fall apart."

Mendoza shrugged. "There's not much routine to do on Buford, when the lab didn't turn anything else. And nothing says it had anything to do with that bar, Jase."

"No," admitted Grace. "But I'd like to talk to some of the people there that night, hang around and meet some of the regulars there. Only of course the owner knows me as a cop. It's a pity Tom was with me—he could wander in all innocent, nobody ever takes him for a cop."

"Well—¡*vamos!*" said Mendoza. "I've got a little idea myself. Oh, that Chard—the anonymous call. I don't suppose there's anything in it, but somebody might ask his wife if he'd had any trouble with anyone lately. He was no loss, however he got taken off."

He sat there for a minute when the men had gone, his mind wandering over Fleming, over the rapes, over the pretty boys. Fleming—there wasn't anything routine could do there. Carey had done it. There'd been a search for a block around, not that there'd be many places in that bare city block where a man could be hidden away, and Fleming couldn't have crawled much farther. Where the hell was the man?

The rapes. Very queer. It would do no harm to ask if somebody at Juvenile had any ideas.

The pretty boys— He roused himself, told Farrell to get him the Mission Church, and found the younger priest there. There would be a requiem Mass for Father O'Brien on Monday morning at ten o'clock.

He got up and said to Farrell, "I'll be over in Juvenile if anybody wants me."

Roy Titus, aggrieved and surprised at having been dropped on so quick, parted with the names of his two pals without much persuasion—Floyd Sporler and Bob Bovers. They were both in Records and Sporler was also still on parole, which made the whole caper all the more stupid. Hackett and Higgins tried Sporler's address first, and found both of them there, trying to get Titus on the phone. They were just as surprised as he'd been, and asked how the cops had found out it was them.

"You ever read detective stories, George?" asked Hackett as they came out of the jail.

"Seldom."

"Fairy tales," said Hackett. "The cunning intellectual criminals. I've never run across one yet."

They stopped for lunch at Federico's and went back to the office. Wanda Larsen was on her way out. She eyed Hackett's notebook and said firmly she was busy, it was her week to qualify at the range. "I'm supposed to be a police officer, not just your secretary, boys."

"So I'll toss you for who types the report," said Higgins to Hackett, and won the throw. But as Hackett stripped off his jacket and sat down, Duke came in with a fat manila envelope.

"Oh, good, I caught you. Understand you were out on this. We're still looking at some of the stuff there, blood types and so on, but I thought you'd like to see this." He opened the manila envelope and spread out a sheaf of glossy black and white 8 by 10's.

Hackett and Higgins looked at them without comment, the mercilessly clear pictures of the carnage worked on the old lady, her place in life. The twisted frail old body was frozen by the camera, its grotesquely smashed-in face, the blood, the bruises, the torn clothes. The little grocery store had been ransacked, cans and packages thrown down from shelves, the cash register opened, but the havoc there was nothing compared to that in the apartment upstairs. They'd seen all this yesterday, after the lab men had been through it; they looked at it again, in the photographs which were somehow worse to look at—a curious effect of timeless photography. The tiny living room with its ancient flowered rug, fat old furniture: the smaller bedroom with its sagging double bed, skimpy carpet, high chest of drawers and chair in golden oak—it had all been ruthlessly torn apart, drawers flung out, upholstered furniture slashed to ribbons, rugs pulled up, the mattress crisscrossed with knife-cuts and off the bed.

"Hunting for the loot, we said at the time," said Higgins. "And it's a toss-up whether it was somebody who knew her reputation—if that was generally known—for keeping cash around, or just somebody picking her at random. And no way to guess what he got or didn't."

"No," said Duke, "but there are points. For one thing, you didn't see the body near to—being good little boys, keeping clear not to spoil evidence for us eagle-eyed scientific types. It was pretty clear she hadn't been dead long when Weinstein found her. The blood was hardly dry. I think she'd just come down to open the store—he said she was usually open by seven-thirty—she was dressed, you notice. And a customer walked in early. Sorry, we didn't pick up any useful latents—the ones on the register too smudged to be any good. But that says to me, when it happened at that time, the odds are it was somebody who'd been living or staying right around that neighborhood, recently. And in the midst of all that mess, there was this." His blunt forefinger came down on one photograph, of the front part of the store. Just beside the front door, a small crumpled object lay on the floor. He removed that photograph and substituted a close-up. The object now showed as a crumpled empty package that had once held cigarettes —Camels.

"Big deal," said Hackett.

"Oh, but you haven't seen this," said Duke. He pulled out another close-up. This one looked as if it had been made under a microscope: the finest details of the little package showed up clear and clean. They could see where it had been torn open from one end across the top, and the blue seal or part of it left, and another seal superimposed.

"By God!" said Higgins. "By God—eagle-eyed, you're damn right."

The little seal, torn across, still showed part of a stamp with black letters. PDL TN PX.

"That's beautiful, Duke," said Hackett. "Pendleton Air Force Base PX. It can't be anything else."

"Narrows it down to whatever personnel has access to the post exchange and wasn't there yesterday morning," said Higgins. "Or come to think, was this thing here when he walked in? What says he dropped it?"

"Don't nitpick, George," said Hackett. "I like it. It's a damned good lead if you ask me. And it makes a picture—him tearing the place to pieces hunting for the loot, after he'd killed her, and then—whatever he got or didn't get—just as he walked out, lighting the last cigarette in the package. That's nice work, Duke."

"I thought you'd like it," said Duke complacently.

"It just occurred to me," said Mendoza to Captain Loomis of Juvenile Division, "on these rape cases we've got—the description the women gave us, just a kid. About fifteen. He won't be in any records complete with mug-shot at that age, but if he's out on this caper that young, it could be he'd given the warning rattle some way before and got into your records."

"That's the hell of a thing," said Loomis. "Rape, at that age? Well, it does happen. We get 'em in here at four and five, budding pros at burglary and you name it—but we can't take pictures either, Mendoza. These days, we're just a sociological counseling service. Let's hear that description again. Well, it doesn't ring a bell with me, but let's ask Melinda and Betty." He opened the office door and beckoned. "Both damn good officers, and they've been here six-seven years, they might have some idea."

Melinda and Betty, both trim in uniform, were respectively black and white, and efficient. They listened to the description, consulted with each other, and Melinda asked, "If he has been in trouble before, Lieutenant, would you have any idea what kind?"

"Not a clue. I only thought he might have been in little trouble before he graduated to big."

"Peter Ricksey?" said Betty to Melinda. "He'd be about fifteen, and he's baby-faced. The last time we had him in was eighteen months ago, for beating up the other kids for their lunch money. He'd fit the description."

"He doesn't sound like the nice polite youngster our victims say he is," Mendoza said with a grin. "Could he act it?"

Betty laughed. "I wouldn't think so. He's completely illiterate, and not very polite by nature. I just can't think of any boy to fit that description, Lieutenant."

"It was just an idea. For all we know, he's never so much as stolen a nickel from Mama's purse," said Mendoza. "But you can see, there's no way to look for him, damn it. Well, thanks anyway."

Palliser, Conway and Landers came up with nine men out of Records to hunt for, by a process of weeding out the ones with suggestive records who lived or had lived on the Central beat and looked something like the Harry Stephanie had described. They went out looking for them, without any conspicuous success.

Hackett got on the phone to Pendleton Air Force Base, and a cooperative sergeant began feeding him long lists of base personnel, military, who had been on leave or otherwise off base yesterday. It was a frighteningly long list. And of course the nonmilitary personnel resident there or having business there could patronize the PX too. Hackett began to feel less enthusiastic about that little clue.

Altogether, Saturday was an unproductive day.

* * *

Saturday night was always busy for Traffic, sometimes
for the night watch at Robbery-Homicide; it varied. Tonight they didn't get a call for some time, and Shogart
amused himself by listening to the Traffic calls—drunk
drivers, drunks on the street, speeders, accidents, one high-
speed pursuit.

"Makes you feel kind of safe here, out of all that mayhem," said Schenke, and the desk buzzed them. There was
a body reported by Traffic.

Piggott went out on it with Shogart. It was an all-night
restaurant on Alvarado, a chain place with a good reputation. The black and white was at the curb, and inside they
found Patrolman Bill Moss and some excited, bewildered
people. It was just nine-thirty, the place wasn't crowded,
but the short-order cook and two busboys had come out
to add to the crowd.

"But, my God, he's just a young guy! It could've been
a heart attack, anybody can have one, but my God—"

"The night manager, Fred Mallow," said Moss. "He
can identify him."

"Identify him!" Mallow was tall and thin, flapping his
arms all around. "His name's Donald Ames, he's only
twenty-three, twenty-four, he works at the tow service down
the street, always comes in here middle of the evening for
a sandwich. A nice young guy, quiet, I just can't get over
this! I can't believe it! Sitting there in a booth, like always,
waiting for Beatrice to bring his sandwich, and all of a
sudden he falls on the floor, and I rush over, and he's dead!
Dead! I can't believe it—"

Shogart was squatting over the body, which lay
stretched out awkwardly between the rows of booths. Ames
was a good-looking young man, dark hair cut short; he had

on a white jumpsuit with red stitching over the breast pocket: *Dick's Tow Service*. Shogart stood up and sniffed, getting out his handkerchief; a minute red stain came off his fingers. "He was stabbed," he said. "Thin blade, right in the heart I'd say. Hardly any blood."

Moss looked surprised; Mallow was incredulous. "Stabbed?" he said. "Why, that's impossible! That's just ridiculous! Nobody came near him! It's early, we're not crowded—you can see, only one couple in a booth, six-seven people at the counter—and he walked in here perfectly O.K., looked just the same as usual, he says to Beatrice, fix me the usual—which is a Reuben sandwich with coleslaw on the side—and he goes into the rest room and comes out again and sits in the booth and lights a cigarette. There wasn't anybody in ten feet of him! Nobody could have stabbed him!"

"I can't help that," said Shogart. "He was knifed." He looked around at the little crowd. "Were you all here when he came in? Then we'd better take all your names and addresses, please."

It took a while; there were ten men and four women, including the restaurant staff. Five people definitely confirmed that not a soul had approached Ames as he sat in the booth, so there wasn't much point in calling out S.I.D. to process the place. It was just another offbeat thing. Piggott searched the body and came up with I.D.—an address in Hollywood. Let the day watch break the news and try to figure out what had happened to him.

They got back to the office at eleven-thirty, and Schenke told them what they'd missed. Roger Perryman, seventy-nine, on the way from the movies to his rented room on Elden Place—his weekly night out. Jumped and beaten up by the thugs. They'd got a dollar and eighty-four cents, left out of his Social Security. Mr. Perryman had been lucky; they hadn't roughed him up much when a squad car came round the corner and they ran off. There were three of them, he said, one with long blond hair and real sporty clothes, he remembered a plaid jacket.

"My God, those punks," said Shogart.

On Sunday morning, Galeano went to early Mass for the first time in years. He hardly knew why he did; he'd got out of the habit, since moving out here away from the family. He went to the nearest church downtown, the old Mission Church, and was surprised and oddly embarrassed to spot Mendoza there, in one of the back pews. He slipped hurriedly out afterward.

And, mulling over Carey's report in his mind, he hadn't got any further about Fleming at all. The other tenants in that building—could there be anything there? Carey had seen them all, and to anyone who knew city people, the results were understandable. That, said Carey, was a place to sleep. There was only one couple, the Del Sardos, people in their fifties, both working. Offerdahl. An old maid in one ground-floor unit, out all day at a job. Two men, Lathrop and Harrigan, both bachelors, also out at jobs. And the Flemings. And the Flemings had only been there a couple of months—the others didn't know much about them, or care. It wasn't the kind of place, they weren't the kind of people, for fraternizing.

Like Mendoza, Galeano told himself that Carey had looked: there had been a thorough physical search for the man all up and down that block. Carey the cynic, looking for the boyfriend, had looked at the single men Lathrop and Harrigan. Lathrop, he said, was a fag: hung out at a

known fag joint uptown. Harrigan had a steady girl friend
he was practically living with.

They said she was homesick. No close friends. She
wrote her family all the time. Galeano wondered—he had
sisters, but he didn't know about females—if she'd have
written home about a boyfriend; he rather thought not, but
you never knew. But there'd be no way to get at those
letters.

Whatever else you could say about Carey, he was a
competent man at his job. So far as the physical evidence
went.

Galeano parked in front of the apartment and looked
at the terrain. The empty house: Carey's men had searched
the yard, all the yards down the block. The newer apartment on the other side was a bare box of a place. The half
block behind, just cleared for a new building, was nothing
but raw earth.

But it wasn't just a physical problem.

He got out of the car, climbed the stairs and rang
Marta's bell. It buzzed emptily at him. She wasn't home.
After a moment he turned and pushed the bell across the
hall.

The door was opened by a little perky-looking gray-
haired woman. He had read all the statements, and somehow he had pictured Mrs. Del Sardo as buxom and dark.
He showed her the badge.

"Oh," she said, "cops again. That really is a funny
thing, isn't it? I've got a theory about it." He saw that her
slate-colored eyes were shallow and foolish. "I think he
was a fake, not a cripple at all. They were going to sue
somebody, he was just pretending to be paralyzed."

Galeano stared at her. "I'm afraid that wasn't—"

"You can't trust doctors, they'll say anything," she told

him. "And if you ask me Mrs. Fleming is a real sly one. Look at the way she made sure I saw them together that morning, her saying good-bye and him in the chair there—"

"You usually leave the same time?" asked Galeano. "It wasn't the first morning you'd seen her leave when you came out too?"

"Well, no, but now I think about it— And then all the fuss and excitement that afternoon— And it wasn't till later I found out from one of the cops, she said she came home at five that day, and it was earlier, and the more I think about it I think there was some kind of plan that maybe went wrong, to cheat an insurance company or something. I thought—"

Galeano fastened on the one thing she'd said. "What do you mean, it wasn't five when she came home?"

"Well, it wasn't. I came home early that day, I know the day because of all the fuss and the cops. I was coming down with a cold, I felt terrible, and the boss said take the afternoon off. So I did, and this place isn't exactly the Rock of Gibraltar"—she laughed—"you can hear neighbors. That Offerdahl! He was never so bad as this before. Anyway, she—Mrs. Fleming—she came home just after I did. I heard her running up the stairs like she always does. Call it two-thirty. And a minute after, down she goes again. So I guess he was all right then, or she was pretending he was. If you ask me he always was all right, prob'ly he's just lying low somewheres. Like I say—"

And what the hell was this? Galeano's mind felt numb. And she added suddenly, "Oh, you got to excuse me, I want to make the eleven o'clock Mass—" She rushed around in her living room (scarcely as neat and clean as Marta's counterpart across the hall) gathering up purse, coat, prayer book; she rushed out past him.

He stood there thinking about what she'd said. Marta

had come home at two-thirty that day. The rest of it was silly, but—

He turned to go down the stairs and faced a nice-looking fresh-faced high-school-aged kid just coming up. The kid passed him and rang the bell of Marta's apartment.

SIX

"MRS. FLEMING'S NOT HOME," said Galeano.

The boy turned. "Oh. Maybe she just went to church. You—you don't want to buy the car, do you? Because she gave me first option on it. That's what I came to tell her, I got the money to pay for it now."

"That's good," said Galeano. "I know she wants to sell it."

"It's a real good deal," said the kid. "A sixty-three Dodge, only sixty thousand on it, for four-fifty. The tires are good too, and it handles O.K.—I've drove it some already. If we can sort of clinch the deal right away, I'd like to."

Galeano said it sounded fine. "Anyway," said the kid, "even if we can't, I want to borrow it again this afternoon to take Mom to Aunt Madge's. Mrs. Fleming let me borrow it before, take her to the doctor's. You a friend of hers? She's a nice lady, isn't she?"

"Oh, yes," said Galeano.

"You suppose she'll be home pretty soon?"

"I don't know."

"Well—uh—my name's Newton. Jim Newton."

"Galeano." They shook hands solemnly.

"There she is," said Jim a moment later as the front

door shut below. "I bet she was just out to church." And remembering Mrs. Del Sardo's revelation, Galeano heard the light footsteps running up the stairs with a leaden heart.

She stopped short on the landing, startled to see them. She wore the hooded coat again, and her tawny hair was spangled with a few drops of rain; just since he'd been here, it must have started again. She had a little purse in one hand, a bunch of keys in the other.

"Hello, Mrs. Fleming. I come by to tell you I can get the car. I already saved up two hundred and my dad says he'll go the rest if I take Mom places in it and pay the gas. Could I maybe take it now? I got the money, if you'll take Dad's check. Oh, Mr. Galeano wants to see you too, but I guess I got here first."

"I have no doubt," said Marta. She came between them and unlocked the door. "It is all right that you buy the car, Jimmy, but now I do not know about the—the legalities, it is registered to my husband."

"If you've got the pink slip," said Galeano, "you can just hand it over, and Jim can re-register it to himself."

"I see. You would know," she said. They had both followed her into the neat little living room.

"You haven't been driving it much, have you, Mrs. Fleming?"

"I have not been driving it at all," she said.

"Oh, I know you had it out a couple of weeks ago, because I came to ask to borrow it and it wasn't here. I just wondered."

Marta turned to stare at him. "I have not driven the car since we moved here. That can't be, Jimmy."

"No, it was gone—honest. It was two weeks ago Friday, I wanted it to take Mom to the doctor's. Gee, Mrs. Fleming, you seen it *since,* haven't you? I mean, nobody's stole it?" He was suddenly anxious.

"Just a minute," said Galeano. "I'd like to hear more about this, Jim. Two weeks ago Friday? You came to borrow the car, and it wasn't in the garage? How'd you know?"

"Well, gee—" He looked from her to Galeano uneasily. "Because I looked. Acourse I knew you'd be at work, Mrs. Fleming, but Mr. Fleming had keys to it. It was raining so hard, Mom said to see could I borrow it because the buses are so bad, so I—but there wasn't any answer to the bell so I thought maybe Mr. Fleming had to go to the doctor or something and you'd took him, so I looked in the garage and the Dodge wasn't there."

Marta was standing very still in the middle of the room. "I do not know anything about this," she said. "It must be a mistake."

"What time was this?" asked Galeano. "You know, Jim?"

"Sure. It was about one o'clock, Mom's appointment was for two-thirty, and I took off from school because of helping her on and off the bus with the cast still on her ankle, see. Say, listen, Mrs. Fleming, you sure it hasn't been stolen, if you didn't know—"

"Let's all go down and look at it," said Galeano.

"This is all very silly," said Marta.

"Come on," said Galeano. They all went downstairs together and down the driveway. It was drizzling very slightly. "You've driven the Dodge, have you, Jim? Trying it out? I suppose, you interested in buying it, you noticed the mileage."

"Sure," said Jim. "The last time I brought it back, it was sixty thousand and forty-one miles. Sure I'm sure of that. I got a good head for figures."

"I wouldn't be surprised," said Galeano. "The key to the garage, Mrs. Fleming?" Silently she singled it out on her ring of keys and gave it to him. He unlocked the padlock and swung open one leaf of the old-fashioned double doors. The old Dodge sat inside. "Let's see what the mileage is." He opened the driver's door.

"Well, there," said Jim Newton, "you can see it's been out since. Sixty thousand and seventy-two miles and four tenths."

"What about it, Mrs. Fleming? Suppose you give Jim the keys, so he can drive his mother—he can come back and make the deal with you later. That O.K., Jim?"

"Sure, sir." Jim's eyes were puzzled on them. Marta gave him the keys. "I hope Mr. Fleming's O.K., Mrs. Fleming."

"That's fine," said Galeano meaninglessly, took her arm and walked her back up the drive. "I've just heard from Mrs. Del Sardo that you came home about two-thirty that Friday, Mrs. Fleming. Not five o'clock as you said. And went out again right away. Why didn't you tell us about that?"

"No," she said. They stopped just inside the front door, in the square little lobby. "No, that is not so. I have told you all the truth."

"And now this comes to light about the car. Kids like Newton know their cars pretty well, and he's sure of what he says. The car was out that Friday, and driven thirty-odd miles. Where, Mrs. Fleming?"

"No. I do not know. It is impossible."

"Do you have a driver's license?"

"Yes, but I have not driven it since we came here. Only to run the engine because of the battery, a few moments."

"Who had keys to it? How many sets?"

She was shaking her head slowly, blindly, back and forth. "No. Edwin had keys, I have keys. Edwin's keys are still here, in the apartment. This is all nonsense, it cannot be."

"I don't think so, Mrs. Fleming. Where were you that afternoon?"

"Ach, *Gott!*" she exclaimed suddenly, violently, and put her hands to her head. "But it is all too much—too much!" She turned and plunged up the stairs, and before he could move to follow her he heard the door bang shut up there. Galeano stood looking after her, his heart strangely heavy, and all he could think was, they were right. The damned cynics. They had been right about her all along.

He drifted unhappily into Mendoza's office to tell him about that, and found Hackett there, one hip on a corner of Mendoza's desk. They both listened to what he had to say, and Hackett commented interestedly, "The same thought, about his faking the paralysis, crossed my mind, but of course there's nothing in it, they hadn't anything to gain and more than one doctor said it was genuine. But this bit about the car, what in hell does it mean? That just makes it funnier, Luis. So she could have driven him some-where—where and why?"

"*No lo niego,*" said Mendoza. "Funny is the word. But she didn't drive him anywhere, if the Dodge was out of the garage at one o'clock. She didn't get off work until two."

"That'd skipped my mind," said Galeano. "But she could have given the keys to somebody."

"Or he could," said Mendoza thoughtfully. "It's a tangle—I don't see through it at all. And talk about things being up in the air—" He had been turning a cigarette round in his fingers and now reached for his new cigarette lighter and pressed the trigger, bent to the flame.

"This Faber thing," said Hackett. "I've been telling him, sometimes S.I.D. hands us the answer right off, but this time all they've done is make more work for us. My God, you should see the list of names we got from Pendleton! Hundreds—and that's only military personnel, there'd be no way to check on all the civilians wandering around, wives and so on. George is feeling pessimistic. He said ten to one that cigarette pack was already there when X came in, but I don't think so. I talked to Weinstein again and he said she was a persnickety old lady, never would have let a thing like that lie around her clean floor. And there was something in what Scarne said—the autopsy will say definitely but they thought she'd been killed just before she was found, and that early in the morning he could have been staying or living right around there. What we're doing now is checking with Pendleton for original home addresses. It's the hell of a bore, but if we do find some airman who hailed from two blocks west of Faber's Market and was on leave to see his sick mother—"

"*De veras.* The routine paying off again." Galeano had wandered out, and Mendoza added ruminatively, "Human nature is a queer thing, Art."

"A profound remark."

"*Vaya el diablo.* That Marta Fleming's a nice-looking girl, nothing spectacular, but to see Nick fall for her—I'll be damned if I can even guess what might have happened there, but if she was mixed up in some piece of collusion to get rid of her husband, I'd be sorry to see Nick knocked out over it. Last man in the world, you'd think."

"I seem to remember you once said that to me," said Hackett dryly, and Mendoza laughed.

"Hard to guess what people see in each other, fortunately for the continued existence of the human race."

* * *

One of the annoyances to police work was that something new was always coming along to interrupt other routine. With the continued hunt for Sandra's killer reduced to the dogged routine, Palliser was now handed this new one by the night watch, Don Ames. It looked from the report as if there'd be a good many people to see, so he roped Conway in on it too.

"I think," he said as Conway digested Piggott's report, "I'd like to see what a doctor had to say about this first. On the face of it, it's another impossibility—by this, he was sitting alone in a booth, nobody near him."

"Let's," agreed Conway. "Though I remember a case, when I was still riding a squad car—"

They found Dr. Bainbridge in his office, conscientious or with nowhere else to go on a rainy Sunday. He said he hadn't seen the body, snorted interestedly over the report, and said, "Humph. I can tell you better after I've had him open, but let's take a look anyway." He led the way down to the cold room and located the right tray; in a morgue the size of L.A.'s bodies tended to pile up. The corpse looked oddly young and defenseless, naked there; and Bainbridge poked at the minute brown line on his left breast, scarcely an inch long.

"There you are," he said. "I can guess what I'll find inside. It was a very thin blade, he probably didn't bleed at all immediately. The witnesses said he'd been sitting alone there about five minutes before he suddenly fell down dead? Typical. He could have been stabbed fifteen, twenty minutes before and not realized it himself."

"I saw a case something like it once," said Conway, nodding.

"It's possible he never felt the knife, didn't know he'd been stabbed. Depending how it happened, he'd have felt a blow on the chest, thought nothing of it."

"That might put it before he got into the restaurant," said Palliser.

"I don't say it was that long, I don't know," said Bainbridge. "I just said it could be."

"Well, thanks anyway." And that was at ten o'clock; Palliser had already been to Ames' address in Hollywood, where he'd lived with his parents, and been through that harrowing scene.

They started out at Dick's Tow Service where he'd worked, and found out from the owner that—as usual, he said—a couple of employees hadn't shown up for the night shift, and he'd been there alone with Ames since five o'clock. They hadn't had a call in an hour before Don went off on his break, and nothing unusual had happened; they'd just been sitting there talking. He couldn't make out what had happened to Don—"I thought a lot of him, hard worker, nice fellow, and he didn't go around picking fights, even getting into arguments. I just can't make it out."

He was a straightforward type, so that seemed to put it right back to the restaurant again, and they looked up Fred Mallow, who was annoyed at being waked up, and heard a firsthand account. "He came in, gave his order and went into the rest room? How long was he there?" asked Palliser.

"Oh, three, five, six minutes—I wasn't watching the clock. Not long. And like I said, he came out and sat down in the booth perfectly O.K., and then five minutes later—"

"All right. Was anybody else in the men's room at the same time?"

"My God, I don't know. I was counting the receipts, I'd just taken over from Powell. I suppose there could've been, but I couldn't say."

"Well, suppose you take a look at this list and tell us

which are employees there and if you know any of the witnesses."

By this time fully awake, Mallow accepted a cigarette and looked at the list of names and addresses. "Sanchez and De Carlos are the busboys. The cook's Bob Smith. Lessee, well, a lot of our regulars I just know by their faces, but I know some of these names. Javorsky, he has the tape and record shop up the block, usually stops in after he closes up. Kravits, he's from the twenty-four-hour pharmacy up the other way, a pharmacist I think. I think I heard this name Cobbler too, if I place him he works somewhere around, comes in pretty regular. This Edna girl, I didn't know her name was Willis, she's from that pharmacy too, been in with other girls, I heard them call her Edna. But she was with a guy last night, I don't know his name, must be one of these others. I'm not saying I don't know these guys, I just don't recognize the names. Michael Jarvis, Joseph Toombs, Tom Sawyer—say, that's kind of familiar at that, wasn't it a movie?"

"Also a book." But they were both common names, thought Palliser. It seemed easier to start out knowing something about the witnesses; and it was going to be a tedious job to get all their stories and fit them together. And if none of them had seen or heard anything significant, where to go on it then? Obviously, none of them—if they were all honest witnesses—had seen anything they thought was important, or they'd have come out with it last night.

"I know we've got to do the routine," said Conway, "but it looks like a waste of time to me. Are we operating on the premise that he got the knife between Dick's and the restaurant booth? On the street or in the rest room?"

"It looks as if that's the only possibility."

"And just as Bainbridge said, never realized he'd been stabbed, or he'd have raised a fuss, hung on to the guy.

He could have run into a drunk in the street, or— But why? There was hardly time for him to've had a fight with anybody, even an argument. Dick said he left about nine-twenty, and Mallow said he was sitting in the booth by about nine thirty-five."

"Well, let's see if we can come up with some answers," said Palliser. They went out separately to find people and ask the questions, and it was a small bonus that it was a rainy Sunday when most people would be home.

Grace had asked Galeano to drop in at that bar and grill sometime, have a look around, get talking to the owner if he was there. He had a bee in his bonnet about that Reinke. Galeano didn't see what good that was going to do, but he wasn't feeling much like going out on a piece of tedious routine, and after a lunch he didn't especially want, he drove up Virgil to Ben's Bar and Grill, parked and went in.

It looked like a quiet family place, the cheerful red-checked tablecloths, and the fat bartender who was probably Reinke was friendly. It wasn't once a year Galeano drank anything but an occasional glass of wine, and of course you weren't supposed to drink on duty, but defying the regulations he ordered a Scotch on the rocks, feeling he needed it.

There was a friendly game of gin going at a rear table, a little money changing hands, but quiet and orderly. He couldn't see there was anything to notice about the place. What they'd heard about Buford, if he'd been in here that night he wouldn't have stayed long: had a couple of beers and left.

Galeano went back to the office and finding Grace there, told him that. "Card game, huh?" said Grace. "Well, I don't get too excited about the state regulations either,

Nick. This thing is going to wind up in Pending. We now know from Buford's bank that he hadn't drawn out any cash in a couple of weeks, and then only fifty bucks. I just had the brother in—he's been through the house and says there isn't anything missing, even his new shotgun there. Which is also funny. Because if somebody intended to rob him, you'd have thought they'd have made a job of it—in for a penny, in for a pound as they say. And then again, the brother said Dick was usually home, and he hadn't been able to reach him for a couple of days. Where was he instead?"

Galeano wasn't much interested in Buford or how he'd come to be taken off. He said, "I suppose I'd better go see that Mrs. Chard again." Not that that was very important either.

He had to look for the address on Constance Street, and by the time he found it, it was raining in buckets. He turned up his collar and dashed for the cover of the deep porch; it was an old California bungalow. Waiting for an answer to his ring, he wondered if Marta had sold the Dodge to Jim Newton; and remembered suddenly—of course, Carey a very thorough man—that there'd been an examination of the car too, and nothing had shown up that was at all suggestive. So what if she had driven the car somewhere that day?

He rang the bell again and thought rather miserably, that part of it could be true. The boyfriend. Edwin Fleming was no good to her as a husband. Say she had a boyfriend, that didn't mean they had to have plotted a murder. There wasn't one scrap of evidence that the man was dead. It was hard to see how he could be alive, but queerer things had happened. And, he thought suddenly, hadn't somebody called Marta straitlaced? If she was just covering up some affair—

The door opened and a waft of noise came out at him. "Thought I heard the doorbell," said the man just inside. "What you want?"

Galeano brought out the badge. The man was little, old, bent over as if he had arthritis or a crooked spine. He said, "Oh. You want Cecelia—it's about Bob?"

"Now what the hell have you got the door open for, you silly old bastard?" Mrs. Wilma Dixon came up behind him, glass in one hand, noticed Galeano, gaped for a moment, readjusted her expression to a winning smile and said, "Oh, it's that police officer who was so nice and understanding about poor Bob. Cissy! You know the funeral's tomorrow, it'll be a great relief to have it over. This is my husband, Mr. Dixon."

"How do," said Dixon, and hobbled away, a hand to his hip.

"Won't you come in?" Galeano went in to a TV turned up too loud in a nearby room, an aroma of port and Scotch. Cecelia Chard appeared in the doorway opposite, gestured at someone behind her, and the TV volume lessened abruptly.

Galeano asked his questions uninterestedly, and Cecelia and her mother looked at each other. "Bob having trouble with anybody? Oh, I don't think so, any more than usual," said Cecelia. "When he was drinking— Why?"

"There's been some suggestion he was deliberately killed," said Galeano absently. "He didn't owe anybody money, or—"

"Oh, I don't think it would be anything like that, Mr. Galeano. He was perfectly all right when he was sober, but when he got to drinking he always got in a fight."

"Led astray he was," said Mrs. Dixon, "by all the bad company he ran with."

It really didn't matter much how Bob Chard had got

himself killed. Galeano thanked them and dashed back to his car through the rain.

Landers and Glasser, out hunting those possibles on Sandra, accepted the rain as an added hazard. Landers was saying that Palliser was being too subtle anyway.

"As far as I can see, Rank is the prime suspect here. The girl picked his mug-shot—sure, with a couple of others, but the same general type—and he's got the right record for the job. He had access to a house in the right area. Well, only maybe, but he looks better than any of these others to me. I say, bring him in again and lean on him, get a search warrant for the house—even now S.I.D. might turn up some evidence of the girls being there."

"Maybe," said Glasser doubtfully. "John saw her, and he's pretty good at judging people, Tom."

They went looking, and of the nine they were hunting found just one at home, in a single room a block away from Skid Row. He had several counts of rape behind him, and except for the goatee he conformed to the description, but how long did it take to shave one off? They brought him in to question when it was apparent he couldn't produce an alibi and seemed nervous. But of course there was nothing conclusive about it, and they let him go. "Waste of time," said Landers.

At least Hackett and Higgins hadn't had to go out on the legwork in the rain. They were still getting fed information from Pendleton Air Force Base, and so far, said Hackett when Glasser asked, they hadn't come across any enlisted personnel who hailed from anywhere near downtown L.A. By some quirk, they hadn't even found any originally from anywhere in California. There must be some, they just hadn't showed up yet.

Landers wandered down to the Records office and

said to Phil, "If you want to take off early, I'll take you out to dinner."

"And what a night for it. I was rather looking forward to getting home, but I'd better take you up on that while you're feeling generous. Not the Castaway—no night for a view."

"The London Grill," suggested Landers. "All quiet and dignified. I'll even buy you a drink."

"It's a deal. I'll just tell the captain I'm goofing off."

They drove up to Hollywood separately. Ensconced in a booth over drinks, it was rather nice to watch the rain drumming down the windows. "I was talking to Margot Swain this afternoon," said Phil presently.

"That Conway. He was afraid she'd get a rope on him. I think he's back to playing the field."

Phil laughed. "Don't worry about Margot. She's mad at him, but there are a few bachelors at Wilcox Street too. She's been dating Bob Laird."

"Good."

"And, Tom, I've been thinking," she went on seriously, "about a house. Before we start a family. While we're both still earning—"

"Hey!" said Landers, alarmed. "The payments—"

"But we'd be investing in something for the future, darling. It's the same as rent really—"

"Phillipa Rosemary!" said Landers. "It's not just the payments, damn it, there's yard work and upkeep of everything and— What?"

"Excuse me, sir, would you care for another drink?"

"Yes," said Landers. "Now look, Phil—"

On Monday morning, his day off, Palliser got up and discovered that it had stopped raining. He reread some of the dog book over breakfast. "It sounds perfectly simple," he said to Roberta. "It shouldn't be very hard with an intelligent dog."

"I'll reserve judgment," said Roberta. The baby began to yell and she added, "Damn," abandoned the dishes and headed for the nursery. Palliser said to Trina, "You're going to be a smart girl and learn all the lessons, aren't you?"

Her eyes and tongue assured him earnestly that she would. He took her leash and put it on; Trina, thinking they were going for a walk, leaped joyfully in circles and got the leash wound around his legs. "No! Come on now." He took her out into the drive, shortened the leash, got her on his left side and said hopefully, "Now heel! Heel, Trina!" He took a few steps forward. Trina stayed where she was. "Come! Come on now, *heel!*" She suddenly noticed the neighbors' Siamese on the fence along the driveway and lunged forward, taking Palliser unaware and nearly pulling him off his feet. "No! Down! Come, Trina—*heel!*"

Ten minutes later, as he urged her patiently to Come and Heel, Trina was lying flat begging to know what she'd done wrong. Roberta said from the kitchen window, "Perfectly simple."

"It takes time and practice, damn it," said Palliser. "You can't expect her to learn all at once, Robin. The book said—"

"Look out!" said Roberta, too late. The Siamese floated down into the driveway with a contemptuous look for a dog on a leash, and Trina took off. Not expecting it, Palliser was yanked off balance and sprawled flat, losing the leash. The Siamese swarmed up the tree in front and Trina began jumping up and down barking.

"You know, John," said Roberta, watching him pick himself up, "I think it might be simpler in the long run if you just asked for Saturdays off so you could take her to that obedience class."

Landers wanted to discuss Rank with Mendoza; he thought Palliser was reaching on this one, when they had Rank under their noses. But the inquest on Sandra was called for this morning, and he'd have to cover that. At least it wasn't raining, and the night watch hadn't left them anything new.

Conway went out to finish talking to the witnesses on Ames, and Hackett and Higgins were still doggedly working through the list from Pendleton. Grace and Glasser started out again hunting the other possibles on Sandra. Galeano hadn't come in yet.

He came in about eight-thirty; he hadn't been able to get to sleep and then when he did overslept. He'd had a funny dream, of Marta driving that old Dodge up a snaky winding mountain road, and always somebody with her, but continually changing to different people: Rappaport, Jim Newton, Offerdahl, little bent-over Mr. Dixon, Conway, Carey, Mendoza. He got up feeling stale and unhappy, and when he got to the office he wanted to talk over this new idea with Mendoza, about the possible boyfriend but no involvement with the disappearance. Whatever else, Mendoza was always acute at diagnosing human emotions. But Mendoza had already gone out somewhere.

"I don't know where," said Sergeant Lake. "The autopsies are in on that bum on the Row and somebody named Altmeyer. And we just had a new one go down— you can take it."

"Oh, hell," said Galeano. But the habit of routine was strong in him, after fifteen years on this force, and he took down the address and went.

It was an apartment over on Commonwealth, and

there was a red truck outside: the paramedics from the Fire Department. They were both leaning on the truck, one smoking, waiting for him. "She was D.O.A. when we got here," said one of them, "but we went through the gestures. O.D. of some kind, just at a guess sleeping tablets—the mother had some, and says the bottle was nearly full. She left a suicide note, the girl." He spat aside. "Makes you wonder, only twenty. Life can be trouble and worry and work, but never a bore, hah?"

"You've got a point," said Galeano. "Where is it?"

"Upstairs, right."

It was a nice apartment, old but good furniture, everything neat except in the bedroom where the body was. There, the paramedics had created disorder, getting her off the bed to work on her. Galeano was gentle with the silent gray-haired little woman who said stiffly she was Mrs. Olson, it was her daughter Nella.

He looked at the body and like the paramedic he wondered. Nella Olson had been twenty, and pretty: a true blonde, neat small features, a nice figure. She'd put on a fancy pink nylon nightgown to die in. There was the suicide note, in a finicky small handwriting in green ink.

Dear Mama, please don't think I am not aware of what I'm doing. It's just that when I know how much more beautiful it is over on the other side, I would rather be there than here. Daddy and I, and Grandma and all of them will eagerly await your coming. Your loving Nella.

Galeano said, "I'll have to take this for the inquest, Mrs. Olson. Do you know what she meant by this? About the other side, and—"

Mrs. Olson said fiercely, "It's all them wicked books she was always reading! There oughta be a law against people writing such awful books! Always bringin' home another one from the public liberry, and even bought 'em she did, good money spent on all them wicked books!" She pointed with a trembling finger. "As the Lord's my judge, if she hadn't read all them awful books, she'd be alive this minute. They oughta put all them writers in jail."

Galeano looked. There was a bookcase under the window, with a good many books in it. Pornography? He bent to look. *Hidden Channels of the Mind, Human Personality and Its Survival of Bodily Death, Noted Witnesses for Psychic Occurrences, Life After Death, You Do Survive Death,* a lot of paperbacks, *True Experiences with Ghosts, Communications with the Dead, Telephone Between Worlds, Strange Spirits, Voices From Beyond.* Galeano didn't know much about this kind of thing, but he recognized one name on several books: Rhine. Respected scientist, he remembered from an article somewhere, not a crackpot.

"All them stories about dead people!" said Mrs. Olson with a sob.

"You don't believe in any, er, afterlife?" asked Galeano, somewhat at a loss.

"Don't you call me no heathen! Good people get to heaven and the rest go to the bad place, but if the Lord'd wanted us to know what heaven was like He'd have put it in the Bible," she said loudly. "All that about dead people talking and it don't make any difference what church you go to and all—it's—it's *unsettling,* that's what, and if she'd never read all them books—"

Galeano might have found it funny, some other day; as it was, he got down names and facts for a formal report, and went back to base to type it up.

Mendoza attended the requiem Mass for O'Brien. He was feeling unaccountably annoyed at Carey, who had foreseen everything. That idle thought about Rappaport as

Marta Fleming's hypothetical boyfriend had now been squashed. Looking back through Carey's voluminous reports, he had found that Carey had already thought of it. Rappaport had a good-looking wife he seemed to be crazy about, and a new house with somewhat astronomical payments. He hadn't been straying from home.

And Marta Fleming was really no *femme fatale*. A boyfriend there very likely was, but where was he? Mendoza had also looked at Jack Frost, and discovered that Frost had for six months been working such odd hours at the Cedars of Lebanon Hospital that it was unlikely he had time to be anybody's boyfriend.

He went up to Federico's for lunch and got back to the office about one-thirty. "Tom wants to see you," said Lake. "He just came in."

"About Sandra," said Landers, hearing him and coming out of the communal office. "I think John's woolgathering. We've got this perfectly good hot suspect, this Rank— the Peacock girl picked him, and he's got the right record. It's a waste of time to—"

Lake swung around from the switchboard. "You've got another rape-assault, in the series, it sounds like. Just an attempt—but what Traffic says, it was the same one."

"*¡Pues vamonos ya!*" said Mendoza. "Let's go! What's the address, Jimmy?"

Like all the other women, she was respectable and matronly: large-bosomed, elderly, slate-colored, indignant. The squad car was still there but they hadn't called an ambulance; she wasn't really hurt. But the men riding the black and whites were briefed on this and that the plainclothes divisions were working, and an alert patrolman had recognized the description.

Her name was Mrs. Alice Drews. "Hurt?" she said,

sitting very erect in an awesomely flowered armchair in her crowded living room. "I didn't take no hurt, after forty years with a man got mean in drink, many's the time I wiped the floor with him, let him know who's boss. I was just a bit surprised, you might say. This little bitty boy asking to cut my grass, real polite he acted, and then askin' for a drink, and bringin' out that knife—but I just lowered the boom on him, little kid like that, and he skedaddled. Only I figured, him tryin' a thing like that, police ought to hear."

"If you could give us a description—" And it would be the same one, unproductive.

"I surely can. It was kind of queer, when I first laid eyes on him I thought to myself, that looks like the Perkins boy from down where I useta live on Stanford Street. I moved here a year or two back, hadn't seen that kid since, but this one surely looked like that Perkins boy," said Mrs. Drews. "But what I recall, he didn't act like him!" She chuckled richly. "That Joey Perkins, he was sure-enough a piddlin' no-account youngster."

SEVEN

"AND WHAT ELSE did I say?" demanded Mendoza. "Only if by some millionth chance one of the women spotted him on the street—I will be eternally damned!"

"You didn't say it was, you said it could be, Mrs. Drews," said Landers dampeningly. "Stanford Avenue, that's not very far from here."

"My Lord, you don't think it *was* that boy? I didn't know the family real good, but they seemed like honest folks, it don't seem likely—not but what that wasn't the first thing crossed my mind when I saw him—"

She didn't know the address, only the block. Mendoza called in to see what help was available, and Grace was there, said he'd meet them. It was the first lead of any kind they'd had on this, and while it was a very thin one, Mendoza was hot to follow it up.

The block on Stanford was a staid and drab middle-class block, mostly of old single homes reasonably well maintained, and a long block. Mendoza started at one end, Landers and Grace at the other; after ringing four doorbells without any result—two eliciting no response and two a couple of housewives who didn't know the Perkinses —Mendoza came out to the sidewalk to see Grace beckoning down the street. They hurried to join him.

"Here we are," said Grace. "This is Mrs. Perkins." He was on the doorstep of a big old white frame place, four doors in from the corner.

"But what do you want?" she asked. "You said you're *police?* We're ordinary honest folk, never anything to do with the police—" She looked it: she was a thin yellow-brown woman, decently clad in a blue cotton dress, thick stockings; the living room behind her looked clean and neat.

"It's about your boy Joey, ma'am," said Grace.

"Joey?" The bewilderment grew in her round eyes. "Joey? You're not trying to tell me Joey's in some kind of trouble? Why, I never had the least worry in the world with Joey—I worried like sin over the others, running around like they did, Johnny wild as a hawk when he was a kid, and the girls—but Joey, never any cause to worry over him, quiet and good like he is. Why, since my husband got killed last year, Joey's kind of been man of the family, last one at home—you aren't telling me—"

"We don't know, Mrs. Perkins, we'd like to talk to him," said Grace gently. "Is he home?"

"I reckon I heard him come in just a while ago—" Reluctantly she turned and called. "What do you think he did, for the Lord's sake?"

Grace just shook his head. "Joey!" she called again. "You come here, boy—some gentlemen want to see you. I'm sure you're wrong, sir—Joey's a good boy, he's had a good Christian raising."

They waited. In a moment there was a shuffling light footstep along the hall, and a boy came up beside her, head down. He might be fourteen, not a very big fourteen. "Let's have a look at you, Joey," said Grace in his soft friendly voice, and slowly the boy raised his head.

"Why, Joey!" said his mother. "What you been up to,

getting all marked up like that?" He had a big darkening bruise on one cheek, a cut on the other, a swollen lip.

"What about it, Joey?" asked Grace.

"Well, I guess," said Joey in a thin treble voice, "it's from where that ole Mis' Drews hit me. I guess you know about that, you're po-lice, ain't you?"

They looked at each other. "Joey, what you talking about?" asked his mother. "You *done* something? Mis' Drews? That lady used to live down the block?"

"Yes, ma'am," said Joey. "I was supprised see her, I was scared she knew who I was. I guess you know all about it, don't you?" And he looked at the men calmly.

They told her they'd have to take him in to question; she protested, just a little boy, there was some mistake. In the end she went along too, and at the office they got Wanda to take charge of her, settle her down with coffee, while they started out talking to Joey in Mendoza's office.

"That's good," said Joey in his reedy voice. "She's gonna be awful upset." He didn't seem unduly upset himself, or sorry for how she was feeling. "I kinda wondered if you'd ever find out about it."

"Would you like to tell us about it, Joey? Just how it happened?" Mendoza had called Loomis of Juvenile; this was one to handle with kid gloves, on account of his age, if there was going to be any prosecution at all.

"Oh, sure. I'll tell you, I'd like to tell you," he said thoughtfully, looking around the office. "The ladies, sure. There was one over the next block and Mis' Walker down the street and about six other ladies I don't know their names, I did the same way, ask about mowing their grass and could I have a drink. And besides the ladies there was a lot of girls, some girls I know in school live right around. I guess mostly they didn't tell anybody about it. I'd tell 'em things like there was a stray kitten back of this billboard and they'd come to see."

"Just hold on a minute." Grace raised his eyebrows at Mendoza. Loomis came in and was briefed. "Now, aren't you making up some stories, Joey? The four ladies we know about. Are you sure—"

"More like nine or ten," said Joey. "I guess just like the girls they didn't all tell, some reason. And I guess I might as well tell you too, I did the burglary at the drugstore up from us. The one on Venice. And another one at the lunch stand the next block, and the store next to it too. And I busted into the school lots of times and broke a lot of stuff. The first day the new teacher was there I took all the money out of her purse, but after that she kept it locked in a drawer."

"Now wait just a minute here, Joey. That's quite a lot you're telling us. Aren't you making some of it up?"

"No, sir. I oughta know what I did."

"*¡Porvida!*" said Mendoza to Grace. "Maybe we'd better get somebody from Burglary to listen to this too. What the hell is all this?"

Before the session was over, they did rope in Burglary, to find that the various break-ins Joey was so readily talking about were indeed in the files, unsolved. "I tole you," said Joey. The only one of the first victims they knew about who was home was Rena Walker; she came in and identified him right away, as did Mrs. Drews. They found the knife on Joey, a big eight-inch snickersnee he said he'd bought at a hardware store. In the intervals, Mendoza and Grace had a long talk with Mrs. Perkins, who was more incredulous than anything else.

"But he's always been such a quiet boy—never got into any mischief! What—what's going to happen to him?"

That was a question. It would be up to the D.A.'s

office; Mendoza and Loomis could make recommendations, which wouldn't necessarily be followed. There'd be the inevitable psychiatric examination, for what it was worth: not much, in Mendoza's opinion.

"But there's got to be a kink somewhere," said Loomis. "My God, I've seen all kinds of the j.d.'s, Mendoza, but this one—you'd think he was talking about snitching a candy bar! Good record in school"—they knew about that then— "and then out of the blue, all this coming out, there's got to be some screw loose there. God knows I don't think any more of the head doctors than you do, but—"

Mendoza picked up his cigarette lighter and regarded it absently. By that time, Loomis had seen it in operation several times, but he still eyed it in a fascinated way as it belched flame. "Reminds me of the story," said Mendoza, "about the social worker doing a research paper on causes of prostitution. When you get past all the broken homes and alcoholism and addiction and weak character, you find some of them just like the life. Somehow I don't think a session with the head doctors will cure Joey of what ails him."

It was past the end of shift when Grace took Joey over to Juvenile Hall and Wanda took Mrs. Perkins back home. And Grace, partly because he was a gentle man and partly because he felt out of his depth with Joey, tried to talk sweet reason to him. "You know you'll have to stay here, and come up in front of a judge, because of all the wrong things you did, Joey. Don't you—"

"Will they ever let me out again?"

"Oh, I expect so, sometime. Don't you feel sorry for doing all these things? Sorry you hurt those ladies?"

Joey turned a thoughtful calm gaze on him. "No, I don't guess I do. I guess as soon as they let me out I'd go do things like that again."

"Why, Joey?"

"Well, I guess I don't know."

Grace turned him over to the Juvenile Hall staff and started home, feeling baffled.

When Piggott and Shogart came on—it was Schenke's night off—they heard something about that from the desk. It was one for the books all right, but in this place, this time, ones like that seemed to come up every week.

Shogart switched on his desk radio to the Traffic calls, put his feet up and shut his eyes. Piggott, reminding himself of several fundamentalist Christian texts on forbearance and tolerance, tried to shut his ears, and opened a new book on the tropical fish. But neither of them had much time to relax on the job; their first call came in twenty minutes later. It was a genuine hit-run, with several witnesses to say so, of course no make on the car, but a dead man and a report to write.

Piggott had just finished writing it when they had another call, a body somewhere on Maryland Street. It was an old house cut up into four apartments, and waiting reluctantly with the Traffic men was one of the upper-floor tenants, Mr. Walter Pepple. "Of all the damned nuisances," he said disgustedly, "this is the damnedest! Now I suppose I got to waste time going in court to tell about it. Just because I happened to be next door. I was tired, I had to do an extra shift last night, I was all in, and these damned people across the hall were like a bunch of hyenas, yelling and laughing—I stood it as long as I could and then I got up and put on a robe to go complain, see, and just about then I hear somebody go tearing down the hall, sure I mean running, and when I go out the door's open and here's this guy bleeding all over the floor—"

He had been indeed, stabbed repeatedly; there was a knife left beside him. Pepple didn't know who he was, said he thought he'd just moved in. There wasn't a landlord on the premises. They found a wallet in a jacket in the closet; if it was his, his name was Rodrigo Peralta. Let the S.I.D. men look for anything else, said Shogart. There were needle-marks all over Peralta's arms; at first glance, and probably at second, it was just another argument between addict and seller, or addict and addict.

They got back to the office at ten-forty, and Shogart had just turned the radio on again when they had a call from the main desk. "Say, I just picked up something a little strange," said Patrolman Bill Moss. "We had a call to a public phone down on Washington, and this guy insisted we bring him here to see a Mr. Galeano. He won't take no, and he's an old guy in quite a state, he won't talk to us, just asks for Galeano, so we thought—"

"Well, and what's all that about? You'd better bring him up," said Piggott, rather intrigued. "Who is he?"

"I've got no idea," said Moss. "I thought it might be something to do with a case, when he knows Galeano. We'll be up." Five minutes later he came in, escorting a little potbellied old man limping and panting.

"Detective Galeano's gone home," said Piggott. "Mr. —er? What is it you want to see him about?"

"Dixon. You just tell him, Mr. Dixon. Seeing it's his fault I damn near got murdered too," said the old man testily, "least he can do is listen to me. I'm staying right here till he shows up, if it's tomorrow morning." He lowered himself into Hackett's desk chair painfully and panted.

Piggott looked up Galeano's number and dialed it. "I don't know what it's all about, but he seems to think you will."

"Dixon?" said Galeano. "Well, I'm damned if I do know, Matt, but I'll come in and find out. I hadn't gone to bed anyway, I'm off tomorrow."

When he walked in half an hour later, Dixon had dropped off to sleep and was snoring slightly, head back. He woke up with a start at Galeano's voice, sat up and grimaced, a hand to his back.

"What's this all about, Mr. Dixon?"

"I had me quite a night, all on accounta you, young feller. Havin' to get out in this damp weather, my arthritis is killing me. Ow. I tried to give you fellows a little hint about Bob, quiet like, and you have to come out flat-footed and say so! Oh, you didn't say it was me on account you didn't know, but them two bitches can add two and two. They knew. How they'd've covered up about me gettin' killed I don't know, because I don't go out and get drunk and pick fights like Bob did, but they was gonna get me—they said so—do me just like they did Bob, beat the poor guy to death they did, I saw it—whangin' away with a couple o' chairs, and that Elmer just a-laughin' all the while they was at it. And they'd've got me too, only for once I was too quick for 'em." He chuckled. "You wouldn't have a cup of coffee around here, would you? I'm still cold as bedamned, that night air."

Piggott went down the hall to the coffee machine. "You mean Mrs. Chard and—" Galeano, even as steeped in sin as any cop of experience, was momentarily startled.

"Who else? Them two bitches," said Dixon. "I'm a patient man, Galeano, but enough's enough. I wasn't no pal of Bob's, but they didn't need to go kill the poor bastard. Just because Cissy found he was runnin' with another woman, for which I can't blame him—and he had a little life insurance too. They beat him to death, the two of 'em, right there in the kitchen, and Elmer got the wheelbarrow from out back and they carted him off somewheres, figure leave him on the street and you'd think he got killed by a car."

"Well, I'll be Goddamned," said Galeano blankly.

"And then, damn it, you had to go and tell 'em there'd been some tip on it, and acourse they guessed it was me! They'd 'a' got me too, but I was too smart for 'em. Locked m'self in the bedroom, and I heard Cissy tell her ma I'd have to come out sooner or later, they'd grab me then— but I got out the window and climbed a fence to the next yard, how I done it I dunno with the way my back's been, but I did, and called up a squad car. And you better believe, Galeano, I don't stir outta the police station till them two bitches and that Elmer, they're all locked up good and tight!"

"For God's sake!" said Galeano. He looked at Piggott and Shogart.

"The statement's enough to go on." Shogart was grinning wryly. "This is his wife and daughter? Well, we'd better go get 'em, and make it all kosher with the warrants tomorrow, get the statement down. My God, what does go on."

They all went out to the Constance Street house, but ended up calling a wagon. The Dixons and Cecelia Chard were all on the way to being drunk, and the two women went berserk. Before it was all over Galeano and Shogart were well marked up by fingernails, Galeano's shirt was torn and one sleeve out of his jacket, and Piggott had the beginning of a nice black eye from Elmer.

"I thought they were riffraff," said Galeano ruefully, "but I never got beyond that. My good God." They had to wake Dixon up again to tell him they were all in jail, and they would see he was driven home if that was where he wanted to go.

"Sure," he said, sitting up and yawning. "It'll be damn good to have some peace and quiet in that house. I only hope some damn fool judge don't let 'em out in a hurry. They'd sure as hell get me good, then."

Mendoza, who had a perverted sense of humor about these things, was still laughing over Dixon that next morning when Conway started out with Wanda to question the Dixons and Mrs. Chard, get statements and warrants. *"Más vale que digan, Aquí corrió, y no, Aquí murió,"* he gasped to Hackett, shoving over Galeano's note. "How right Nick is, if you don't get rich at this job you get a look at human nature. *Dios mío,* the people we meet. And how are you and George doing on your private hunt?"

"We're not. Nothing suggestive's turned up at all. I'm beginning to think George is right, that cigarette pack could have been there for weeks, maybe she just didn't notice it. We'll go on to the bitter end, but I think it's a waste of time."

"Which I understand," said Palliser, passing Hackett in the doorway, "Tom's been saying about my brainwave on Sandra. What do you think?"

"You talked to the girl," said Mendoza consideringly. "From what I know of the case, Rank could be a hot suspect. Why don't you think so?"

"For one thing, he was at work out in Van Nuys at that car-wash place up to three o'clock that Sunday. I don't think he'd have had time to get to Hollywood and pick up those girls by five o'clock. He's not the only man in Records with the right pedigree and possible access to a house near San Pedro."

"And we aren't even sure of that, are we? But the girl picked him, John."

"Along with a couple of others. Damn," said Palliser suddenly, "we never did locate that Steve Smith. Who she also picked. But she wasn't at all certain, you know, and I think myself the fact that these mug-shots showed men wearing goatees had something to do with her picking 'em. At least I understand we've got those rapes cleaned up—Jase called to tell me about it last night. My God, what a thing."

Sergeant Lake buzzed Mendoza. "You've got a new one. Twenty-fourth Place, double homicide."

"*¡Diez millones de demonios!*" said Mendoza. "All right, I'm on it, Jimmy."

They went to look, and they looked sadly: just more of the mindless brutality stalking the streets of any big city. The daughter had come home from a night at a girl friend's and found them: Mr. and Mrs. Paul Freeman, both in their fifties, beaten and dead on their living-room floor and the house ransacked. A modest house, but between sobs Janice Freeman told them this and that. "Of c-course we were always careful about locking doors and all—there's the chain on the front, you can see. Not that Daddy ever had much money himself, but there's the church money—he keeps the books for our church, the Methodist chapel it is, and he always had the collection to take to the bank— Oh, if I'd only been here, if I'd just been here—"

If she'd been there she'd probably have ended up dead too. There were a few suggestive things to notice. Mendoza nodded at the phone book, lying open on a table against the wall, oddly undisturbed. "The door wasn't forced, chain off. That could be why, John."

"Oh, yes," said Palliser, going closer to look at it. The book was open to the yellow pages, to the listing for service stations. "He rang the bell—or they did—said he was stalled and could he please use the phone. And the helpful Christian let him in."

"*Tal vez.* You'd better call up S.I.D." Looking at the corpses, Mendoza thought about statistics. They did enter the picture. Thoughtless people would quote the fact that the incidence of black crime was astronomically higher than white; what they forgot was that there was an astronomically higher number of black victims too.

"Oh, if I'd just been here. I can't help feeling it wouldn't have happened if I'd just been here—"

Galeano got up late, his day off, dropped his jacket at a tailor's for repair, and drove down to the Globe Grill for breakfast. This time he sat where Marta had to wait on him. Her lips tightened when she saw him, but she came up correctly to take his order.

"Did you sell the car to Jim?" he asked.

"Yes," she said stiffly. "That is all right? There's no reason I should not?"

"Not that I know of." He ordered almost at random, and she went away at once. She didn't make any comment on his facial decorations; maybe she thought cops were always getting into fights. She didn't come back until she brought his plate, and he watched her unobtrusively. Damn it, he thought, the girl was nothing to him; just, those damned cynics so ready to believe she was telling a tale, and he—halfway—believed her. He was sorry for her; look at it any way, she'd had a raw deal. And if she was telling the truth— But there were all the questions: her coming home earlier than she'd said she had that day, and the car, what that Frost woman said, what they'd said about Fleming—

Damn it, why should she tell such a story unless it was true?

He wondered suddenly if Carey had thought of digging up that raw empty lot where the building had been torn down. That was woolgathering with a vengeance. For one thing, he thought suddenly, Mrs. Del Sardo was right —that place had thin walls, you couldn't have a good argument without neighbors knowing it. It didn't make much noise, say, to hit a man over the head, but a little girl like Marta couldn't have got him out of the place, down the stairs, alone.

What about the wheelchair? It had rubber tires. Galeano had a sudden clear vision of Fleming, dead or dying, tied into the wheelchair while she manipulated it down the stairs quietly, so quietly, late at night. She'd taken him to the doctor—that had meant getting him down the stairs. She was a sturdy girl, and it was a question of leverage, keeping the thing straight. But he'd probably helped, those times, with the increased strength in his arms and shoulders.

That was nonsense too. She couldn't have done it; there hadn't been time. He'd been perfectly all right that morning when she left. And the boy said there'd been no answer to his ring at one o'clock. And the car was gone then.

Galeano gave it up. Only God knew what had happened to Edwin Fleming, and He was preserving inscrutable silence.

Jason Grace had three exposures left in the Instamatic, and used them up that morning taking pictures of cuddly brown Celia Ann, who was—impossible as it seemed— nearly eighteen months old now. She was pretty special to him and Virginia because they'd waited so long for her, deviling the County Adoption Agency.

"You want anything at the market, Ginny?" he asked after lunch. "It looks like rain again, and I think she's coming down with a cold."

"She can't be after all the shots. Jase, you've got that look again. You're thinking about something, and you know I wanted to go see your mother this afternoon. Are you going out on something on your day off?"

"Just around a little, Ginny." He brushed his mustache back and forth. "I just had a little idea."

"Your little ideas I know," said Virginia. Grace grinned at her and picked up the phone. When he got hold of Robert Buford in Thousand Oaks, he said after identifying himself, "I hope you're feeling better, Mr. Buford."

"Well, I suppose. It's over. That is, the funeral's tomorrow, we had to wait till your office released the body."

Grace didn't bother to correct that to the coroner's office. "I've got a funny sort of question for you, Mr. Buford. Did your brother like to play cards? Gamble a little now and then?"

"That is a funny one, Mr. Grace. Well, he used to. He used to be quite a man for that, years back. But Mary, his wife, she disapproved of it and he hadn't for a long while. Tell you something funny, Mr. Grace—when I couldn't get hold of him, it just crossed my mind to wonder if maybe he'd gone down to Gardena, one of the gambling houses, to sort of pass the time. He was at loose ends, and since Mary was gone—but I don't think he would have, at that. He'd got out of the habit."

"I see. That's interesting," said Grace.

"You found out anything about who killed him yet?"

"Not yet, but I may have a little lead," said Grace.

"Thanks, Mr. Buford. . . . Ginny, I'm off. I'll be back sometime." She just gave him an exasperated look.

He dropped the film off at the drugstore and went on downtown, to Virgil Avenue. It was just one-thirty. Ben's Bar and Grill was open. The little idea might be nothing at all, but in Grace's experience you had to, as the song said, accentuate the positive to get any results. It was said that if you sent a telegram saying *All is discovered* to any ten people at random, nine of them would pack bags and start running. He believed it.

He walked into the place and went up to the bar. The owner, fat bald Charles Reinke, was alone here: no customers yet. He recognized Grace with a nod, obviously remembering the badge in his hand before. "Do for you?" he asked unwillingly.

"Oh, Scotch," said Grace. "Straight up. By the way, why's it called Ben's? Your name is Charles."

Reinke looked even more wary at the implication that Grace had been checking into him. "Uh, it was named that when I bought it," he said. "It'd been here awhile, I just didn't bother to change the name."

"Sounds sensible," said Grace, and sipped Scotch. "But you know something, Mr. Reinke. I don't need to tell you that the state examiners are pretty damn choosy who they sell liquor licenses to. You could lose yours right away quick if they got to hear you're running illegal card games here."

"Oh, hell and damnation," said Reinke. "Hell *and* damnation. I knew it—I knew it'd get around, those God-damned fools— It wasn't my fault! I didn't want any part of it! I told them to go away somewhere else, I told them about my license, listen, this place is all I got, I just barely make it now, I got to keep my nose clean if I—I told them!"

He was nearly wringing his hands; he looked at Grace anxiously. "How did you hear about it? Have you—have you—"

"Called up the board and said come grab your license quick? No, Mr. Reinke." Grace hadn't anticipated this reaction; from what Galeano had said, he'd rather expected the quiet game in a back room with a cut to the house. "I don't think the regulations are just very realistic myself." It was a human instinct, gambling. Reinke's fat face looked somewhat less miserable.

"Neither do I—I don't know your name." Grace told him. "—Mr. Grace. But there they are—and I get caught with customers playing for money, I'm dead. Look, it was only the once, see. I asked them to go somewhere else, I told them, but Sam—he just laughed and said I shouldn't worry so much. I couldn't do nothing about it, because—" He hesitated.

"Good customers?" suggested Grace, letting him take his time.

"Well, yeah, but also—I might as well say, as long as I got to tell about it—also, I owe Sam some money. I got in a bind last summer when my wife was sick, we don't have any insurance, and Sam loaned me a thousand. I been payin' it back as I can, but he's been a damn good friend to me, he's a nice guy and I just didn't like to press it, he brought out the cards. Honest, it was only the one time and I'll see it don't happen again."

"All right," said Grace casually. "When was it? Was Dick Buford in on it?"

"Yeah," said Reinke, passing a hand across his mouth. "Yeah. That was another reason I felt kind of nervous, you coming before, asking. I suppose it was just a coincidence, him getting clobbered by some thug just after, but—"

"That night? Last Tuesday, a week ago today?"

"Well, no," said Reinke. "No, it got started on Monday afternoon. They just got to playing and sort of kept on. It was draw poker."

"Mmh-hm," said Grace. "Who was in the game?"

"Well, Sam—Sam McAllister, he lives down the block on Fifth. He started it, and the Colombos—Rudy and Vic Colombo, they own the garage across the street, got a couple reliable hands so they could take the time off. And Andy Bond, he's a regular too, a retired guy like Sam. There was another guy, I'm not sure of his name, he works at the men's store across the street, but he was only in the game awhile, said he had to get back to work. Then Buford dropped in, late Monday afternoon, and got in it. I asked 'em to go away, they could go to Sam's, but Sam said his wife'd kill him if she come back, find the place in a mess—I guess she was away somewheres—and they were comfortable here, everything to hand like, and I shouldn't worry. I could just go home, he said, he'd keep count of any drinks they had and sandwiches and all, and if they got tired they'd lock up. But they didn't," said Reinke. "They was all still there Tuesday, all Tuesday, and I was wild, I tell you."

Grace marveled slightly, no gambler himself, but he knew such sessions did go on. "Sam's nephew was with them then," said Reinke, "young sailor, he was on leave, stayin' with Sam. Yeah, Buford was still in too."

"When did it break up?"

"Along about seven that night. I told them they had to go away, I didn't like it. And I guess by then they were getting tired, no wonder, even if one or the other'd drop out awhile and lie down in my back room. They finally broke it up and went."

"Would you happen to know who came out ahead?" asked Grace. "They playing very high stakes?"

"I don't think so, but it went on so long— Yeah, Buford and Andy took kind of a bundle, I guess. I remember this sailor sayin' they'd got most of his shore-leave money, and Sam said maybe he'd got some education for it, better than spending it on girls."

"They all left about the same time?"

"About. I was damn glad to see them go, and I made up my mind, Sam try that again, it's no go—I'll put my foot down. Mr. Grace, you aren't going to do anything about it, are you?"

"Not to you," said Grace, finishing his Scotch.

The sergeant at Pendleton had been very helpful, but Hackett was tired of this damned job. He and Higgins had by now come across several military personnel stationed at Pendleton who hailed from California, but nowhere near L.A.

"And that," said Higgins finally with a long sigh, "is that. *Finis*. If it was a hunch, it was a dud, and damn Scarne and S.I.D. We might better have asked Luis to consult his crystal ball."

"Probably." Hackett lit a cigarette and flipped over the sheets on his desk. "Oh, damn—here's one we missed, George. The AWOL's. But it's short and sweet— And isn't that a coincidence?" he added suddenly. "Don't speak too soon. Here's an enlisted man, Leo Mullarkey, AWOL last month. His home address is on Magnolia, just a block away from Faber's Market."

"And I suppose he made for it right off," said Higgins, "the first place they'd look for him."

"People do stupid things or we wouldn't have such a good reputation," said Hackett.

"I believe you. I said to Mary, I think the stupidity rubs off on us. I don't know, I suppose it is just barely possible, Art. And wouldn't you know, if he is, the last one of all these hundreds of names. But he won't be there now, for God's sake."

"Maybe we can get an idea when he was." Hackett got up and put on his jacket. Higgins straightened his tie.

Palliser, who had been typing a report across the room and just picked up the phone, said suddenly, "You don't say, Jase. Who? Well, I'll be damned! The boss'll be interested in that, but I'll never understand how anyone can waste time over— Yes, I see. Yes, it doesn't say how much but we can talk to the other men and— You and your little ideas. I'll pass it on. . . . Jase just came across something interesting on Buford, Art."

"Buford? Oh, that. I hope we've just come across something interesting too," said Hackett.

Outside, it was making up its mind to rain again. They took Higgins' Pontiac, as it were for good luck. They couldn't transport a subject in Hackett's Barracuda.

The address on Magnolia was an old square stucco house with a strip of brown grass in front and an ancient Ford sitting in the drive. They parked in front, went up and rang the bell. After an interval the door opened.

"Mrs. Mullarkey?" Hackett showed her the badge.

"What the hell do cops want?" She stared at them angrily, unwilling acknowledgment in her eyes of two great big cops, looking like cops, on her doorstep. "Oh, I suppose you're lookin' for Leo—we don't know where he's at." She was a fat bleached blonde about fifty, makeup plastered on, in tight black pants, a bright flowered tunic.

"When was the last time you saw him?" asked Hackett.

"Listen, the soldiers come and asked—*and* asked," she said impatiently. "We ain't seen him since—I coulda told them Leo wasn't goin' to stay at one thing long, and he never did like bein' told what to do, no way. So he took off from the Army, so what? How did we know that, or figure it was some big crime?"

"He was here?" asked Higgins.

"Look, I told that sergeant or whatever he was, sure, Leo landed here, God, I dunno, way time gets away from you, it was about three weeks, a month back—he says he's on leave, he only stayed overnight, he said he was goin' up to 'Frisco. That's all I know."

Hackett and Higgins looked at each other and shrugged. Dead end. It could be that in the short time he was here Mullarkey had sold or given some cigarettes with that PX seal to somebody around here. He could have stayed right around here and been the X they were hunting. That was probably as close as they were going to get.

But Higgins had caught the one word. "You said we, Mrs. Mullarkey. Your husband could back that up?"

"Husband!" she said, and barked a laugh. "Just all I can do take care of myself, without some lazy man. I got shut of him years back. It's enough I got two no-good boys, bring the cops down on me. But I got to say, Billy's got some feelings, not like Leo—believe it or not he gives me some loot just the other day, though where the hell he got it I don't know and can't say I care, the way money goes these days—"

"Billy?" said Hackett. "Is he here?"

"Last I looked, watchin' TV and drinkin' the last o' my beer. Cops!" said Mrs. Mullarkey bitterly. "That damn Leo! Always makin' trouble—I could wish I'd never married that bum—" She stared resentfully at them as they came past her into the house.

Billy Mullarkey was a big beefy young man in stained T-shirt and jeans, sprawled in an armchair wolfing pretzels and beer, watching a game show. He stared up at Hackett and Higgins, and the badge momentarily mesmerized him.

"How about it, Bill?" said Hackett. "Leo gave you some cigarettes when he was here, didn't he? You had them on you when you decided to find out if it was so, old Mrs. Faber kept lots of money around? You were up early, weren't you? About seven-thirty that morning, you walked in there, she was just open, and you—"

"What the hell are you talkin' about?" asked Mrs. Mullarkey.

Without saying a word, Billy stumbled up to his feet and ran blindly for the door. The two big men were more than a match for him, and wrestled him down before he got there. He began to swear, and then he started to cry, and as they hauled him up to his feet and got the cuffs on he sobbed, "It was all her fault, Goddamn it! I wouldn't 'a' hurt her, but she wouldn't tell me where all the rest was— a lousy forty-two bucks I got—if she'd 'a' told me I wouldn't 'a' hurt her—it was all her Goddamned fault—"

EIGHT

AFTER THEY GOT HIM into the car they asked if he'd make a statement, and he said he wasn't going to say nothing more, embellishing that with various obscenities, so they took him straight down to the Alameda jail. They had enough to get a warrant, and it was to be hoped the charge would stick. After it was passed to the D.A.'s office it was out of their hands.

They got back to the office, nearly at the end of shift. Palliser and Conway were in, nobody else. "It almost had to go back to the restaurant," Conway was saying. "The time element. So this says so all over again, John. Between us we've talked to all the other witnesses, and what the hell do they all say?"

"The boss here?" asked Hackett.

"Oh, he took off." Palliser grinned. "Jase had a bright idea on Buford, and when I passed it on our Luis went all absentminded and wandered out—having the same hunch Jase had, I gather. I expect we'll hear about it. Rich thinks we've got somewhere on Ames, which would be gratifying."

"Well, what did we hear?" Conway flung himself back in the desk chair and lit a cigarette. "Talk about nebulous! Which wasn't surprising, when Ames himself didn't know he'd been stabbed, apparently. They said they didn't notice him at all, or just casually saw him come in and sit down— a couple of them recognized him from seeing him there before, didn't know him—why should anybody have noticed him? But the night watch got all the names and addresses down, and there they are all present and correct to talk to, until I come to this Tom Sawyer. Address turns out to be an empty lot. And all I say—"

"Yes, and I'd agree with you," said Palliser. "It's too late to do anything about it today, but I think we get back to Mallow on it, and see if Piggott or Shogart can give us any description. You look self-satisfied," he added to Hackett. "Been doing any good?"

"Breaking a case. The Faber thing. Routine does sometimes pay off. What was Jase's little idea?"

"Interesting," said Palliser thoughtfully. "At least our Luis thought so."

Mr. Sam McAllister was about sixty-five, tall and angular, with a few wisps of gray hair. He was retired from the personnel department of The Broadway department store. He was regarding Mendoza rather sheepishly, and he said, "Now how'd you come to hear about that?"

"Mr. Reinke was annoyed," said Mendoza, grinning back at him. "Never mind. Did you do any good?"

"Well, Millie was annoyed too," said McAllister, involuntarily looking over his shoulder toward the kitchen where an emphatic banging of pans betrayed Millie's presence. This was a neat little stucco house in the middle of an old block of neat homes, minute lawns in front. "Not too bad, I come out a little ahead. Lordy, but I don't know when I've done such a thing, not in years. We all kind of got carried away, I suppose. Old Charlie fussing about it being illegal—guess he had a point. Tell you one thing, I was bushed when I got home that night—not so young as I used to be!" He laughed.

"Your nephew was in on it too, wasn't he? Reinke said, a young sailor."

McAllister nodded. "Young Ted Nygard, my niece's boy. Dropped a little too—I was sorry about that later. He just joined up a while back, green kid from the farm, it was his first leave out here. He's on a cruiser, real proud of it." He added the name; he looked at Mendoza with some belated caution; at first he'd just been glad of an audience. "Did I understand, you're with the state board, something to do with Charlie's license? Lordy, he did say something, but I just never thought—I sure hope you aren't going to blame Charlie. It was all my fault we got started, come to think."

"Well, we'll overlook it this time," said Mendoza casually.

"I wouldn't want to think I got Charlie in any trouble," said McAllister.

Mendoza looked at him, the simple and honest—and rather stupid—old man. "You needn't worry about that, Mr. McAllister."

"That's good. Oh, Lordy, there's Millie—don't like to rush you off, but she likes to be regular with dinner—"

"I was just leaving." Mendoza clapped on his hat against the slight mist; it was already dusk, and trying to work up to rain again. He was going to be late home.

The night watch came on, and not long after Shogart had switched the radio on Mendoza called. He wanted the phone number of the captain in Harbor division. "I think his name's Noble, Matt. I'll hang on."

Curious, Piggott consulted the main desk and passed it on. "Now what's that about?" he asked Schenke.

"Couldn't say. Look, E. M., tune that thing down, will you? Both of us rode a squad long enough it's no novelty, you know." Shogart glowered at him but complied.

They got their first call at nine-twenty, a heist at a seven-to-eleven dairy store on Hoover. The young fellow alone in the place was scared green; it was only his second week on the job. "I mean, one thing I thought when I took this job," he said to Piggott, "it's not like a liquor store, a drugstore, where you're liable to get held up! My gosh! A dairy store! I mean, it's crazy."

"A lot of things are these days. Could you tell me what he looked like?"

"My gosh, no! He had a ski mask on, covered his face, and a cap—I couldn't say anything except he was big, about six feet. He got all the cash, about sixty bucks."

So there wasn't much to do about that but write a report.

When Mendoza came into the kitchen Alison was sitting at the table, hiccuping over coffee. The cats were weaving around her feet, and in the backyard the twins were galloping around with Cedric and Mrs. MacTaggart in pursuit.

"Children!" said Alison with loathing. "Hic! Those little devils know they have to get ready for—hic!—the school bus, why they have to make so much trouble for M—oh, damn!" She leaped up and fled for the bathroom, and the cats dispersed in all directions, El Señor spitting furiously.

Mrs. MacTaggart came in, herding the twins before her breathlessly, and he said, "You don't think there's anything wrong, Mairí? I know what the doctor said, but—"

"Ach, doctors!" said Mairí. "She'll be fine in a bit,

it's just she didn't expect it, having it easy the first time. That bus will be here any minute and these two heathens not washed—there's coffee on the stove—"

"I'll get breakfast out, Mairí." He dodged Cedric slurping from his bowl on the back porch. He backed out the Ferrari, but didn't head downtown.

It was nine-fifty when he walked into the office of Captain Noble of Harbor division and asked, "What about it?"

Noble was a hardbitten middle-aged man, big and stolid. "Well, I've got him here for you," he said. "When you called last night I checked with the Shore Patrol and found he was aboard all right. We picked him up this morning, about an hour ago, after a little argument with the chief petty officer. What do you want him for, Mendoza?"

"I don't know that I want him for anything," said Mendoza. "It's just a little hunch. And when I checked with the Navy and found the ship was still in port, I thought I'd better talk to him while I could."

Noble shrugged. "He's in an interrogation room down the hall. Ready to chew nails and talking about his rights as a citizen."

"Lead me to him."

When he went into the little room and shut the door behind him, Ted Nygard swung around belligerently. "Who the hell are you and what the hell's this all about?" He was about twenty, a good-looking youngster with crew-cut blond hair and a pink and white complexion, trim in his blue uniform. "What is all this, anyway? Police—"

"Lieutenant Mendoza, Robbery-Homicide. Sit down, Mr. Nygard. I've just got a few questions for you." Mendoza laid down his hat, got out a cigarette and contemplated him consideringly. "You were on leave about a week, ten days ago. You went to stay with your uncle—or great-uncle—Mr. McAllister, up in L.A."

Nygard flushed, to betray his youth. "My mother asked me to go see them," he muttered. "I was only there a couple of days. Why?"

"You got into a hot poker game while you were there, at a little neighborhood bar."

"You're Goddamned right I did!" said Nygard. "Bunch of silly old bastards like Uncle Sam, I thought, and it turned out, I guess I was the sap—they cleaned me out! Not Uncle, he dropped some too, but this one guy was stacking the deck, I could swear. He walked away with a wad, mostly mine." He looked at Mendoza more warily. "But so what, what's your business with me? Did you say—"

"The poker session, Mr. Nygard. Was this fellow's name Buford? And you thought he was ringing in a cold deck? Naturally you were annoyed." Mendoza was filling in gaps, and it was easy to do. "You went home with your uncle that Tuesday night, and he was tired and went right to bed—but you were still missing your money. You went out again and found Buford's place—mmh, yes, I could guess. You knew his name, and that he lived in the neighborhood—he'd be in the book. Yes, it's one thing to lose money legitimately, but when you thought he was a sharp—"

"Hell!" said Nygard, flushing deeply. "Did he lay some kind of charge? I wouldn't think he had the nerve! All I wanted was my money back. Yeah, I found the place, the door was open and I went in and he was sound asleep in front of the TV. If you know so damned much—"

"But he woke up when you started to search him for the money," said Mendoza, "and you had a little scuffle."

"Well, damn it, I didn't want to hurt him," said Nygard, "he was a lot older than me, but I wasn't going to let him get away with that loot, and I told him so. Did he lay a charge on me? Damn it—"

"No," said Mendoza, "but I'm afraid we're going to. He's dead, Mr. Nygard. We won't be calling it Murder One, but he got knocked down and cracked his skull and died of it."

Nygard lost all his pink freshness; he stared at Mendoza in dismay, incredulity. "Oh, no," he said, "I just gave him a little push—I didn't even hit him—I thought he'd knocked himself out and I just—oh, my God! I never meant a thing like that—my God!"

Mendoza got back to the office just after lunch, and met Duke coming in. Hackett was alone in the sergeants' office, laboring over a report. Mendoza told him about Nygard: Harbor division would send him up to be booked in, and there'd be the statements to get, the warrant to be applied for. It was Higgins' day off, and everybody else was out on something.

"And what have you got?" he asked Duke, sitting down at his desk and reaching for the flame-thrower.

"The first report on these Freemans." Duke spread out glossy 8 by 10's. "The autopsies'll give you more, but provisionally we think they were attacked by at least two men. They don't seem to have made much effort to defend themselves, as if they'd been taken by surprise, both struck down at once maybe. I don't think they had a chance. There was the usual mess, and not much there to get—it was raining, and there were some muddy footprints on the hall carpet, but not distinct enough to make anything of." The photographs were just as usual too, not very pretty. "But you called our attention to the phone book, and we

took a little trouble there—lifted a very nice set of latents."
Duke sounded smug. "All four fingers, for a wonder.
They've just gone down to R. and I., if we've got him on
file we'll know who one of them is anyway."

"Bueno," said Mendoza. "You'll let us know. Where
is everybody, Art?"

"Out. John and Rich got some kind of lead on Ames,
and nobody'd done much on that addict who turned up
dead, Peralta. Nick had an inquest to cover."

"The Olson girl. That was *muy extraño,"* said Mendoza, and Sergeant Lake buzzed and said the D.A.'s office
wanted him. It was one of the juniors, and he wanted to
talk about Joey. They didn't feel it was a case to prosecute
formally, and to save time and money a reduced charge
would probably be brought. The D.A. would be interested
in Robbery-Homicide's opinion about that; it would really
be easier all round if they simply put him away as incor-
rigible, in which case—

"In which case," said Mendoza sharply, "he'll be automatically released when he turns into a legal adult, with
no charge on his record. I wouldn't go along with that
at all. He's exhibited a good deal of violence, and very
likely the minute he's turned loose he'd continue to do so."

Well, the D.A.'s office felt it wasn't worthwhile to do
anything else. They had quite a case-load here, as Mendoza
knew.

"¡Qué demonios!" said Mendoza to Hackett. "What
do you bet that kid will be out and roaming around with
a knife again before he turns eighteen? The trouble we go
to, and then the damned lawyers—I swear I'm going to get
out of this rat race! And somebody's got to get those statements on Buford, Art."

"I'm going, I'm going," said Hackett hastily. As he
went out, Mendoza had opened the top drawer and brought
out the deck of cards.

* * *

"Tom Sawyer," said Fred Mallow blankly. "Outside of the book, I never heard of one." He looked at Palliser and Conway. "But I said I didn't know everybody in that night."

"Well, we can try to narrow it down some," said Conway. "You knew most of the people by sight if not name, no? O.K., between us Sergeant Palliser and I have seen all the rest of them, except this bird who gave us the phony name and address. So let's start from scratch—"

Mallow yawned again, looking puzzled. "I don't see— oh, I get you. Maybe we could at that. You figure it was this guy, whoever he is, stabbed Ames? I still don't see how anybody did." They had waked him up again, but he was ready to be cooperative.

"All right, the ones you know by name and looks first." Palliser handed him the list. Mallow checked it off obediently: four people, three men and the girl, Edna Willis. "You didn't know the man with her, but we do, having talked to him—Michael Jarvis. Who was there you knew by sight and not name?"

"Jesus, I'd have to think back—lessee, there's a guy about forty, sandy hair, thin, comes in two-three times a week, wears sports clothes usually. Usually in about nine."

Palliser looked at Conway, who said promptly, "That'd be Adrian Forbes. He lives at the hotel around the corner."

"And there was a guy in work clothes, young, long hair dirty blond, about six feet. He's been in before, not regular but I recognized him."

"Ralph Ensler," said Palliser. "He drives a *Times* delivery route. I talked to him."

"That's it," said Mallow, looking at the list. "These others, I don't know the names. Toombs, this Sawyer— Pace and Woods. But, say, where's—"

"Forget about everybody else but Sawyer. The others are O.K., we've talked to them. Now, the big question is, what does Sawyer look like? This is a secondhand description, Mr. Mallow, and you may not place it even if you'd seen him before." Considering all they knew now about Don Ames' reputation, it seemed hardly conceivable that anyone had had a grudge on him, deliberately sought him out; but you never knew. "You remember it was our night watch came out on it. We've talked with the two officers and tried to get anything they remembered about the witnesses." It had been a roundabout way to do it: the witnesses had been just strange faces to Piggott and Shogart, but on the other hand they were trained to notice faces. And it could be that this shy witness had defeated his own purpose with the false name, because it had caught Piggott's attention as he took it down, and remembered more about the man.

"Well, shoot," said Mallow obligingly. "I'll see what he sounds like."

"The best we can get, he was on the young side, between twenty and thirty, medium height, stocky, with light hair going thin, and glasses," said Palliser. "He might have been wearing a tan jumpsuit."

Mallow stared. "Why, that's Georgie," he said. "I just now noticed on this list, Georgie's name isn't here and he was there that night. I saw him talking to the officers when they were taking names. You don't mean it was Georgie who—"

"We don't know. Maybe he was just shy of giving police his name for some reason," said Conway, his gray eyes hooded. "Georgie who?"

"George Little, he works at the Shell station kitty-corner from the restaurant. But Georgie wouldn't do a thing like that! I don't know him except as a customer, but he seems a very decent guy." Mallow was troubled. "I can't make out why he should give a wrong name."

"Well, we'll hope to find out. Thanks very much, Mr. Mallow."

They weren't feeling certain that this was going to provide an answer. People did foolish, impulsive things for all kinds of reasons and no reason: it was just a lead that had to be followed up. As they left the apartment building where Mallow lived, Palliser buttoned his coat and said, "I don't know when we've had so much rain in January."

"Probably mean an extra-hot summer," said Conway. They were using his Buick. They made the eight blocks to the little chain restaurant quickly, in the middle of the day, and Conway slid into the left-turn lane, crossed and pulled into the Shell station.

A young kid came up, long hair falling over his eyes, and said indolently, "Yuh?"

"Is George Little here?"

"That's him over there." The kid jerked his head at a broad back bent over the raised hood of a car away from the pumps.

"O.K." Conway pulled to the side of the apron and they both got out. "Mr. Little?"

The man straightened and turned. "That's me," he said; and then he saw the badge in Palliser's hand and stood very still. "Cops."

"That's right. Is there somewhere where we can talk to you? The station—"

"Sure," said Little dully. He was mechanically wiping his hands on a rag, over and over. "Sure." He tossed the rag away and turned to the little glass-fronted station; they followed him in. "I bet I know how you found me," he said. "It was a damn fool thing to do, give you guys a wrong name. Fred Mallow knew I was there." And of course one small annoying thing about it was that they needn't have gone the long way round; if they'd shown the list to Mallow he'd have told them right away who wasn't on it and should have been.

"That's right. Why did you do it?" asked Palliser.

Little sat down on the edge of the desk. "Because I was scared," he said in a low voice. "I didn't believe it, when Mallow went over and said he was dead. I just didn't believe it. But then when the squad car came—and they said we all had to stay for the detectives—I was scared. I just wanted to get away." He raised his eyes briefly.

"Why?" asked Conway.

"Ah, you know why." He was silent, and they gave him time; he made several false starts at it, ran oily fingers over his thinning hair, and finally said, "The whole thing don't make any sense at all. I don't know why it happened. Yes, I do, but it was—it wasn't—I don't know. See, there's this girl. She goes out with me sometimes. I—that night, I wanted to call her, but not from the station, I—the boss— he don't mean anything but he likes to kid people. I went over to the restaurant on my break." He was talking expressionlessly, head down, as if under a compulsion to explain just how senseless it had been. "There's a public phone just outside the rest rooms, down that little hall the other side from the counter. I'd just got up to it when I found out I didn't have any change, and this guy came up just then, this Ames—I didn't know his name, I'd seen him there before. And I asked him for change for a dollar, and he gave it to me and went into the rest room. So I called Dorothy—I still had the rest of the change in my hand—only she wasn't home, her sister said she was out with somebody. And I was, I guess, so mad and kind of upset about it, I just stood there, and then I looked at the change in my hand and it was only eighty cents, he'd short-changed me a dime. And then he came out and I told him so, and he said he hadn't, and I was still mad, I put the change in my pocket and there was my knife—" He brought it out slowly and showed it, an only slightly over-sized pocketknife with a white handle. "It's a gadget," he said, and pressed a catch on the top to fold and unfold the blades, one long and one short, very thin and pointed. "I did it before I knew I would, just like a little kid—I—I—just wanted to hurt somebody," he said. "And I never thought I'd really hurt him—I called him a name and he looked kind of surprised and then just went by me, and after a minute I came out and sat at the counter and had some coffee. And then—over in that booth— And Mallow said he was dead! I swear to God, I thought he'd had a heart attack, it couldn't've been what I— And then that one big plainclothes cop said he'd been stabbed. I couldn't believe it." He raised his head. "You'll arrest me now, I guess."

"That's right, Mr. Little. We'll want to get all this down in a formal statement."

"Me, killing somebody. I still can't believe it," said Little. "All right, I know you got to. I better call the boss to come in. That snotnosed kid can't fill a tank without falling over his own feet."

What with one thing and another, not much had been done about Rodrigo Peralta, the addict found knifed on Monday night. Landers had started out to do some legwork on it, had talked to Walter Pepple and failed to find the other two tenants at home. They had turned up a record for Peralta, a petty pedigree of narco possession and B. and E., and that had given them the address of a relative, an uncle, Rubio Gonsalves. Glasser hadn't found him yesterday, so now Landers tried the address again, down on Santa Barbara, and found him home. He was sitting in his single room, clad in underwear and slacks, reading a Spanish-language newspaper. He listened to Landers impassively and said, "The boy is dead? Let God judge him. He was nothing to me any more."

"You don't know who any of his friends were?"

"No sé. Nor I did not care. He had chosen his own road." He shrugged massively and picked up his paper again.

It didn't seem to be the best moment to tell him that the coroner's office would come down on him to pay for the funeral. Landers went downstairs again, into the dirty, dingy city street where refuse blew down the sidewalks and collected in the gutter, to where he'd left the Corvair down the block. It had begun to rain again, rather hard. He got into the car, and the engine was dead, wouldn't even try to turn over. Landers said a few things, got out and looked under the hood, decided it was hopeless to do anything in the rain. He found a public phone, called the auto club and huddled in the overhang of a building for thirty minutes until the tow truck came.

The driver had a look at the Corvair's innards, slammed the hood and said, "She'll have to go in, mister. She's about had it. Good little car, but a car's only good for so many miles, you know. You need practically everything new. Oh, sure, a garage can fix her up, but it'll only be a question of time before she goes out again."

Landers said a few more things. "Well, tow it in to the agency," he said. "I'll talk to them about it."

He called a cab and got back to the office in the middle of the afternoon.

Hackett had just got back to the office at five o'clock, after getting the formal statement from Nygard and starting the machinery on the warrant. It was pouring rain outside, and he was wet. He found Landers blowing off steam about his car to Glasser, who said they'd all been telling him to trade that thing in for a year.

"Phil thinks it's so funny," said Landers. "Saying I'll have to break down and buy a new one, and my God, it isn't that I'm stingy, but the payments—"

"Get a Gremlin," said Glasser. "You'll get damn good mileage."

"I know, I know, I've driven Phil's."

"Oh, Sergeant Hackett! Listen, I gotta make you believe me this time, they're—"

"Oh, for the love of God!" said Hackett disgustedly. Mr. Yeager had plunged through the doorway with Sergeant Lake in pursuit.

"You've gotta listen, they're gonna do it tonight, they're gonna murder that woman! I heard 'em planning just how to do it, they're gonna hit her on the head and put her in the bathtub and make it look like an accident, like she slipped and fell, and—"

"Now, Mr. Yeager," said Hackett. "If you're going to tell me you were in the hall again and the door was open, don't. Why don't you just try to forget about it—"

"—And the girl's going off after she's helped him, see, nobody knows he's got a girl, his ma, Mis' Lampert, she's kind of jealous of him—and then he'll pretend to find her and act all sorry and cry and carry on—"

"Now listen, Mr. Yeager. Just calm down. Try to explain to me just how you heard all this. You know you can't. You're just imagining—"

Yeager took a step back, licking his lips and looking in despair between Hackett and Lake. Then he said sullenly, "Oh, hell. Well—well, if you gotta know, I—I got the place bugged."

"What?" said Hackett. Landers laughed.

"I—well, hell, I don't have much to do, nights," said Yeager weakly. "I took a course in electronics once. I—I did it first, we had a couple sets of newlyweds in the place—" Lake and Glasser began to laugh helplessly. "And it was kind of interesting, and—well—well," said Yeager half defensively, "it was, you know, kind of like picking a channel on TV—"

"What the hell's going on here?" asked Mendoza, coming across the hall to find all his available staff convulsed with merriment and Yeager standing in the middle looking miserable.

Hackett pulled himself together and told him, and Mendoza began to laugh too. "It's not so funny!" said Yeager. "It was—you coulda knocked me over, I heard 'em talk about it the first time—and damn it, I tried to get you to believe me, so you'd stop 'em, but you wouldn't pay no attention! And I knew I hadda do something, so I— I got all the rest of it down on tape. The other times they talked." He reached into his pocket and produced three cheap sixty-minute tape cassettes. "Now you gotta believe it!"

"Well, I will be Goddamned!" said Hackett. "If this isn't one for the books—you mean that innocent-looking fellow is really— Damnation, and we'll have to do something about it." He looked at his watch. "I'd better call Angel. Luis?"

"I wouldn't miss hearing those tapes for a million bucks," Mendoza said, grinning.

The tapes would make excellent evidence; this would be one trial that wouldn't cost much time or money. They went out with Piggott and Schenke to surprise the quarry, and they did. Mendoza had laughed over Mr. Yeager's homemade entertainment; and in the course of twenty-six years at this sordid job, he had seen violence and blood, tragedy and death, brutality and mayhem of all sorts, but he wouldn't soon forget the look on Mrs. Lampert's face as she listened to what they knew, how they knew it. Looking from them to her son—a little too good-looking, Edward Lampert, with a weak chin and pale eyes—she aged twenty years in a moment. Expectably, he blustered and was sullen in turns, but finally parted with the girl's name, Diane Ashley, and her address. Hackett went to add her to the party, and collected some fingernail scratches to match Piggott's.

They ended up at the jail at eleven o'clock, booking them in.

"But you know, Mr. Yeager," Hackett had said before that, "you'll really have to remove all the bugs. Apart from anything else, it's invasion of privacy."

"I guess so," said Yeager. He sighed deeply. "I'm sorry it had to come to that, I hadda tell you, get you to believe me. But I guess I better. But you just got no idea, Sergeant Hackett—it was interesting as hell!"

About two o'clock that morning Patrolmen Zimmerman and O'Neill were handed a call to a disturbance on Alvarado. When they got to it, they found an interested little crowd, mostly black, around a couple outside an all-night restaurant, beside a car at the curb.

"You take him in and lock him up!" the woman shouted at them as they got out of the car. "He tried to kill me! Tried to strangle me!" She was a young woman, not bad-looking and decently dressed. They calmed her down and she gave them a name, Ruby Blake. "I just stopped in that place, have a bite to eat before I go home after work—I work at a rest home, night shift. He got talking, acted all nice and polite, and offered me a ride home. And then when I got in his car, he started fooling around and tried to strangle me!" She was crying then, and she opened her coat to show them a couple of darkening bruises.

They couldn't get anything out of the man at all. He was light-skinned, clean-shaven, about thirty: looked ordinary. He just looked at them sullenly and wouldn't answer questions. They looked in the car and it didn't have any registration, so they called in the plate-number. It had been reported stolen in Beverly Hills that afternoon.

"Would you make a statement charging him, Miss Blake?" asked Zimmerman.

"I surely would! You just tell me where to do it. Treat a decent girl like that—"

"It'll be assault with intent," said O'Neill. "Robbery-Homicide."

"The night watch has gone by now. Leave a report with the main desk," said Zimmerman, "and stash him in jail." They called the garage to tow the car in and put him in cuffs and drove down to the Alameda facility. He never said a word all the way.

The day watch had hardly come in, on Thursday morning, when there was a heist reported at a drugstore on Spring Street. Galeano went out on it, and the pharmacist gave him a good description. He was so mad, he said he'd come over right now and look at mug-shots. He did, and within five minutes of the time Phil Landers had settled him down with a book, he picked one. "That's him!" he told Galeano positively. "I'd know him anywhere, that ugly mug! He didn't even have a hat on, I'd know him in the dark!"

It was a picture of one Adam O'Hara, and he had the

right record for the job: two counts of armed robbery and a few other things. There was a fairly recent address, and Galeano went looking for him. It was a small apartment on Sunset Avenue, and he got no answer to his ring, but the door across the hall opened and a nice-looking little gray-haired woman asked, "Are you looking for the O'Haras?"

"That's right," said Galeano. "Do you know where Mr. O'Hara is?"

"Why, yes. He'll still be at the hospital. He said he'd let me know, but it's a first baby and I expect she'll be some time. What? Oh, it's the French Hospital. He was so worried, poor boy, I had to call the doctor for him."

Galeano went over to the French Hospital and discovered Adam O'Hara in beaming transports over a fine boy, nine pounds three ounces, born twenty minutes before. A whole staff of nurses, nurses' aides and other prospective fathers could say that O'Hara had been there since two o'clock that morning.

Galeano was annoyed, and for some reason he also felt queerly desolate. Even as Mendoza said about the citizens, *They have eyes and see not.* It was likely that the pharmacist, angry and excited, had mistaken O'Hara's mug-shot for somebody who looked like him—he wasn't an unusual type—but Galeano hadn't any immediate impulse to browse through the books looking.

It was raining now in a halfhearted sort of way. He went to have lunch at the Globe Grill, and Marta wasn't there. He sat where she would have waited on him, but the buxom dark girl came up instead. He waited till she brought his order and asked, "Isn't Mrs. Fleming here?"

"No, she's off sick." She hardly looked at him, didn't seem to recognize him as one of the cops who had been here.

Galeano ate his macaroni and cheese, not thinking

much. Come down to it, Carey and the rest of those damned cynics had done all the thinking on it. All from the old viewpoint, drilled into any cop as any lawyer, what was the crime, who profited, how was it done, by whom.

Damn it, he felt sorry for her: and maybe he was being stupid. He could follow the way Mendoza and Carey thought, logically—and there were questions to be answered about Marta Fleming. But he found that sometime just in the last couple of hours he had come back to simple feeling, and what the feeling said was, that's an honest girl, telling the truth. And if that was simple in another sense, the hell with being too smart.

He paid the bill, put on his coat, went out and drove down to Westlake Avenue. He had to turn to park on the legal side. The place was quiet except for a faint hint of singing in a whiskeyish voice, from the top floor.

He pushed the bell; pushed again. After a while the door was pulled back and she stood there. She had a navy wool robe belted tightly around her, and her russet-blonde-tawny hair was uncombed, her nose red.

"Mrs. Fleming—"

"You!" she said. "Police again! Am I never any more to have peace?"

"Now listen," said Galeano. "I—"

"*Gott im Himmel!* Go away!" she said furiously. "I do not wish to talk to you—is that for you enough plain language?"

Galeano began to feel slightly irritated. All the various things the people he'd talked to had said about her slid past his mind. "If you'd just listen—"

"I will not listen to you, stupid pig of a policeman! Go away!" she said arrogantly.

Galeano, that mild and even-tempered man, quite suddenly lost his temper. He reached out and took her by the shoulders and shook her hard, back and forth. "Who's stupid, you damned silly woman? It's no wonder you haven't made any friends here, keeping your damned stiff-necked pride, never meeting people halfway! All I wanted to tell you, damn it, is that I believe your damned silly story—I think you're honest—and God forgive me for maybe being a fool! Now if you want to go on being a Goddamned martyr, it's perfectly all right with me, but all I can say is, I think you're a bigger Goddamned fool!" He shook her again and let her go and stepped back.

"Oh!" she said, and for a minute he thought she was going to hit him, and then she crumpled against the door-frame and began to cry in great gulping sobs. "But I am not a martyr—all my fault—because I was weak—and nobody, nobody, nobody to talk—*sehr einsam, niemand*— *Ach, die kleine Kätzchen, die kleine Kätzchen, aber*—all my fault—*ach, so richt,* I cannot talk with people, tell how—" She fell forward, sobbing, and Galeano caught her in his arms.

NINE

HE WAS ALARMED. She was sobbing so hard her whole body shook, and she made strangling noises in her throat. He half carried her over to the couch, and she lay huddled over one arm uttering great gulping sobs. He didn't know what to do; he'd never seen anything like it.

"Hey," he said uneasily, "are you all right? Marta?"

Gradually the sobs lessened in intensity; she shook with several long shudders, half straightened up, put her face in her hands, and then after a long moment she sniffed, groped in her pocket for a handkerchief, and blew her nose. She was still shaking a little, and she said in a muffled voice, "I am ashamed. I am sorry—to lose control so—"

"Don't you feel better?" asked Galeano.

She blew her nose again. "Yes, I do," she said, sounding surprised. "It—it is not easy that I—"

"Everybody needs to let off steam once in a while," said Galeano. "You just kept it all bottled up too long."

And surprisingly, Marta suddenly laughed—a wobbly and half tearful laugh. "You are so very right," she said. "It has been—what's the phrase—one damned thing after another."

Galeano was so relieved he laughed too, uproariously.

"You'd better tell me all about it. Maybe I'd understand better. You know, what you need right now is a good stiff drink. It won't do your cold any harm, either."

"Yes, I have caught a cold. There is a bottle of brandy, I was going to mix it with some lemon—"

"The hell with the lemon." Galeano went out to the kitchen, found the brandy, poured her a stiff four fingers and gave himself a smaller one. "You get outside that, and if you talk some you'll feel better yet."

She drank a third of it at once, took a long breath, shuddered and sat back, closing her eyes. "I am," she said dreamily, "very tired. I think you are a kind person. You see, I cannot help but feel it was all my fault—all my fault." She drank more brandy. Between that and the sudden flood of expended emotion all her reticences were down, overrun. "Because I never should have married him. I never loved him as a wife should. It was wrong. We learn too late."

"Why did you?" asked Galeano.

She looked at the brandy, her dark eyes brooding. "My father—he owned a small manufacturing business in Lingen, our home. It was prosperous, we had thought there was money—there was always money, we were not very rich but my sister and I were not raised to work at jobs, at the convent you don't learn shorthand, typing. Then Papa died, and it seemed there had been speculation, he left my mother nothing. Oh, the building was worth something, the land—that is all. I had to find work—Elisa was too young then." She finished the brandy. "There was an American unit stationed near, the girls go out with them, and a girl I knew introduced me to Edwin. He asked me to marry him. I did not love him, I liked him well enough is all. My mother said it is the best chance I will ever have, in America there is always opportunity and he is a good honest man. She is very old-fashioned," said Marta, smiling a little, "and she said love is not everything in marriage. I saw all that for myself—and so I married him."

"And it didn't work out?" asked Galeano.

She gave a short laugh. "Oh! Yes, it worked out, as you say—the way such marriages do! He was not an educated man, but he was good and kind—he was clever with his hands, and a hard worker, he might have made much of himself, gone places as they say. After I had the baby, I felt reconciled—*meine kleine Kätzchen*. But she died— so soon, she died. The doctor said, a thing wrong in her heart, she would never have lived long, but— And then Edwin was hurt in the accident, and those doctors said he would always be so, an invalid, helpless, in the wheelchair. It was like a nightmare beginning, and it does not end. There was no money, no compensation for him—I do not understand all that, but we had a lawyer—that cost a great deal of money too, I still owe the lawyer money, and it all came to nothing. He needed a great deal of care. It was then I began to think, all my fault, for I should not have married him, feeling no love for him. I try to be a good Catholic, I knew my duty, to look after him as a wife should. He was of no faith, we were not married in the Church, but one takes vows nevertheless. But it was hard. Oh, for him too! I realize—but it was difficult."

"And then—what did happen that day?" asked Galeano. "Three weeks ago tomorrow?"

She opened her eyes and put one hand to her temple, slowly. "Mother of God, have I not asked myself?" she said quietly. "We had come here, because the rent is much cheaper and I can walk to work. In that way, it was better, but not all ways. He had been very despairing, ever since the baby died, and he had said to me many times, he would be better dead, such a burden on me and no good to anyone. I had been afraid he would kill himself. It would not be a sin to him perhaps, but to me—I had come home, several times since we are here, to find him drunk. That terrible old man upstairs—he would come, pretending sympathy, and bring him whiskey. I tried to talk to him, ask him not to do so, but it was no use—no use. And then— there was that day." She was silent, and unobtrusively Galeano tipped the rest of his drink into her glass. She finished it absently. "It was such a very usual day to begin with. I left for the restaurant. I had got him dressed and into his chair, given him breakfast. The woman across the hall was leaving also. And then, when I was at work, I remembered my letter. The last evening I had written a letter to my sister Elisa, I meant to take it to post, and I had forgotten it. I was going shopping, to buy her a birthday present, but I wanted to post the letter."

"So you came home to get it," said Galeano, and let out his breath in a long sigh.

"Yes. I was in a great hurry—it has been easy to blame myself for that too—I had to catch the bus up to town, there would not be much time to look in the shops before they closed, and I must be home to get dinner for Edwin before I went back to the restaurant. I did not even look to see where Edwin was—when he was not in the living room I thought perhaps he was lying down, he could get to the bed from the chair—and I did not even look. I took up my letter from the table there, put it in an envelope and left again, for the bus. And I went to the post office—we cannot afford the air mail, it is expensive enough to send by sea—and when I had shopped for the present I came home. And I told you how it was. He was gone. His chair was here, and he was gone."

"You remember if the wheelchair was in the living

room when you came home the first time? But you'd have noticed that—"

"It was not. His coat is gone also," said Marta. "I think I have had too much brandy."

"His coat. Regular topcoat—raincoat?"

"A good thick wool coat, brown. He bought it in the east before we came here. And there is another queer thing. I am talking too much to you, but it does not matter." She laughed a little drearily. "What thought did I ever have for money, until Papa died! But now, it is always to think of money. So always, I have a little, what I can save, hidden away for the emergency. I had not looked at it, since Edwin was gone, until last week. And it is gone too."

"I'll be damned," said Galeano. "How much?"

"Two hundred and eighteen dollars," she said, shutting her eyes again.

"Where was it?"

"In one of the kitchen jars—canisters, the one for sugar."

"Be damned," said Galeano. "Did he know it was there?"

"Of course. He was my husband."

"Well—" Galeano looked at her. "You do feel better, don't you? Do you good to get all that out of your system. I'm sorry I swore at you."

"But I called you names too." She smiled a little. "And after you said you believed me, too. I think you've been kind. But right at this moment, nothing seems to matter to me so very much."

"Never mind," said Galeano. "Part of that's the brandy and part the cold, I expect. Things will matter again. And I'd better go—I've got a job too. You take care of yourself, is all. Listen, things are going to get better."

"Do you think so? I wonder."

"They've got to," said Galeano stoutly. "You just take care now."

And he was of two minds, as he got into his car downstairs, whether to pass all that on to Mendoza.

Palliser had been the first man in that Thursday morning and Sergeant Lake gave him the message relayed up from the desk last night about the assault-with-intent lodged in jail. "Something else," said Palliser. But it had to be followed up, so he went out again and over to the Alameda jail. The suspect had refused to give a name and was booked as John Doe. When one of the trusties brought him to an interrogation room, Palliser said, "Sit down. Have you decided to tell us who you are?"

The man sat down opposite him and said reluctantly, "Steve Smith."

"That's a step further on," said Palliser mildly. And that was interesting. The Steve Smith they'd looked for last week? He was clean-shaven, looked younger than thirty-three, but the rest of him conformed to the description. Palliser had been thinking of this as just another routine errand, but now he looked at Smith with covert interest. "Why did you attack that girl last night?"

"I never attacked nobody. She's a liar."

"Had you ever seen her before?"

"No."

"You just got talking to her in the restaurant, all casual?"

"She made up to me," said Smith after some thought.

"Oh, is that so? Did she ask you to drive her home?"

"Yeah. Yeah, she did."

"All right, what happened then?"

Smith thought some more. Then he said, "Well, we

got in the car and she said I should, you know, love her up a little. Then when I tried to she yelled and got out and a couple fellows grabbed me and called the pigs. I didn't do nothing to her, that girl. She's a liar."

"She had a couple of bruises where she says you tried to strangle her," said Palliser.

"I never. She's a Goddamn liar."

Palliser offered him a cigarette, lit it, sat back and lit one himself. He said conversationally, "I see you've shaved off your little beard."

Smith was startled; he jumped in his chair and said, "How the hell did you—I never seen you before in my life!"

"Oh, we have ways of knowing things about you," said Palliser vaguely. "Where were you a week ago Sunday, Smith, do you remember?"

"A week ago—I don't know. Somewhere around. I don't remember."

"Where have you been living?"

"Room over in Hollywood."

"Got a job?"

"I been lookin' for one. I been on unemployment. Some new rule they got, you got to come in ever' day, wait for a job to show, or they don't give you no pay. That's where I been, days."

"I'll bet," said Palliser, "I could tell you when you shaved off that goatee. It was—"

"I got a right to shave if I want."

"Sure," said Palliser. "But you did it right after you killed that girl, didn't you? When the other one got away and you were afraid she'd finger you?"

Smith leaped up out of his chair. "You don't know that! You can't say that!"

"I just did. That was when, wasn't it?"

"No, it wasn't. I don't know what you're talkin' about, man."

"We both know what I'm talking about, Steve. You picked those girls up at a lunch counter on the Boulevard, a week ago Sunday. You ended up raping and strangling one of them."

"I never did no such thing!"

"—But you made a mess of getting rid of the body," said Palliser. "It didn't burn, you know. The fire went out."

"Thass a Goddamn lie," said Smith, "I seen all the smoke it made, like—" and stopped.

"So, suppose you tell me where you took them," said Palliser gently. So many of the ones they had to deal with were stupid punks like Steve.

"I'm not sayin' anything else."

"Oh, yes, you are. Just a little more. How did a bum like you happen to have a house to take them to?"

"I ain't no bum. I said I been lookin' for a job. I still had a key to it," said Smith sullenly.

"Where is it?" asked Palliser patiently.

"Listen, I didn't mean to hurt that girl none. She, just like this damn woman last night, she said I should love her up and then she yelled—I didn't go to—"

"Where, Steve? You might as well tell me, we'll find out in the end," said Palliser.

He came back to the office at noon. "And I hope to God S.I.D. comes up with some solid evidence," he said to Mendoza. "We haven't been exactly brilliant on this one —I really didn't think that Stephanie girl knew what she was talking about—but at least we got there in the end. It was a strictly spur of the moment deal—"

"With the ones like Steve, they usually are," said

Higgins, who had been sitting at the other side of Mendoza's desk when Palliser came in.

"*Ya lo creo.* So what did he tell you, John?"

"He'd been down here visiting an old pal a couple of days before, and noticed the house was vacant—his mother used to live there, and he still had a key. When he picked up the girls it was the first place he thought of. He got some groceries on the way—there was a refrigerator there, the place was furnished. I'll bet whoever owns the place will be surprised to get a power bill. It's on Gladys Avenue."

Mendoza grunted. "Three blocks from San Pedro. Very nice. Let's hope S.I.D. turns something."

"I just turned them loose on it."

And Lake came in with a telex: the feedback from the FBI on the prints picked up in the Freeman house. Mendoza swore, looking at it. "Why can't these hoods stay home, George? New to us—his record's all in West Virginia. Neal Benoy, and he's wanted for homicide, and that's all they tell us. Well, we know he's here, or was, but it'd be helpful to know something more about him. Jimmy, get me an outside line." After an interval, he got connected to a Lieutenant Devore of the Huntington force, and began taking notes. Devore gave him the gist of Benoy's record.

"He's been just another no-good bum around town till he got together with a kindred spirit one night last August and murdered a harmless old black fellow. We picked them both up, but they made a break on the way to the courthouse for indictment. I wouldn't be surprised if they were still teamed up—they're buddies from way back. You want Benoy for something out there? A long way from home—he's never been out of the state before, far as I know."

"We've tied him to a double homicide," said Mendoza. "The lab thinks it was a pair. Who's the other one?"

"Tony Allesandro. Birds of a feather," said Devore succinctly. "You want his prints and particulars too?"

"Anything you can give us."

"I'll shoot some stuff out."

"*Gracias.* We'll get an A.P.B. out on both of them, just in case." Mendoza put the phone down. Higgins and Palliser had gone out, and Galeano had just come in, looking thoughtful. He sat down in the chair beside the desk. "Have you recovered from your aberration, Nick?"

"Damn you," said Galeano amiably, "it's not. I said all along that girl is honest—if she wasn't, she'd have thought up a hell of a lot better tale than that. I just want to put this in front of you—" and he plunged into the story of Marta's revelations. Mendoza sat back, smoking.

"From the viewpoint of human emotions, *interesante,*" he said sardonically at the end, "but as for giving us any clue to what happened to Edwin, damn all."

"I know, I know. But it does show why she'd thought and done things to look suspicious. All perfectly natural," said Galeano.

"Maybe."

"And maybe you think she's conned me!" said Galeano.

"Not necessarily. But I would damn well like to know what did happen to him," said Mendoza. "The hell of it is, the pair of them were so damned isolated—no close friends, the other people in that place strangers, and she—"

"Homesick," said Galeano. "Proud. Holding everybody at arm's length. I hope she'll learn better."

"And I've reluctantly come round to admit, at least, that there isn't any smell of a boyfriend," said Mendoza sadly. "It shakes my faith in the eternal venality of human nature."

"They do say, it's the exception that proves the rule. I just thought you'd like to think all that over," said Galeano, and went out.

Mendoza sighed and swiveled his desk chair around to stare out the window toward the Hollywood hills, invisible today in heavy gray mist. Every now and then something a little more complicated than usual showed up. As a rule the things that baffled them were just the anonymous crimes (like that dairy-store heist) where no possible lead showed and there was nothing much to be done about it. But once in a blue moon, a real mystery came along, where there should be leads and weren't; and the mystery of Edwin Fleming was the most baffling one that had come their way in some time. He missed Hackett, off today, to talk it over with.

At five o'clock Palliser and Glasser came in with Scarne. "Well, we've got Sandra all tied up," said Glasser. "These stupid jerks—Smith trying to get rid of the body and he couldn't even do that efficiently—you wouldn't believe the stuff he overlooked at that house. It's still empty, luckily, nobody in to mess up the evidence for us. The first thing we found was Sandra's green plane case. There were prints all over the house—"

"We had the Peacock girl's and Sandra's, we've sorted out quite a few of both," said Scarne. "Odds and ends of clothes the parents can probably identify, but the prints are solid evidence. He isn't going to be able to claim that Sandra ran off and met up with some other X, the times are too tight. The other girl could say she was alive at seven, and the autopsy says she was dead between eight and ten."

"Good—solid evidence I always like," said Mendoza.

"And something new just went down; we passed George and Jase going out in a hurry," said Palliser.

Landers had heard what the mechanic had to say about the Corvair without much surprise. The damn thing had been on its last legs for months. "You'd do better to junk it," said the mechanic. "It's not worth putting money into."

Landers took a look at what they had on the used lot, but nothing looked like a good buy. He walked on down Hollywood Boulevard to the American agency, priced a couple of new models and winced, and went out to the used lot to browse around. Finally he settled on a little Sportabout, the pony-size station wagon, and made a deal for it. It was only three years old, had thirty thousand on it, which wasn't bad.

But at least the Corvair had been paid for. What with the new payments on top of the rent and everything else, he reflected, Phil would have to stop talking about a house for some time.

Higgins and Grace looked at the new homicide and had the same thought at the same time.

"The Freemans," said Grace, touching his mustache thoughtfully. "Same earmarks, George."

"Such as there are," said Higgins. This was much the same kind of house as the Freemans', in the same kind of neighborhood: modest middle-class. The householder had been Mrs. Myrtle Hopper, widow, who'd lived alone here since her youngest daughter got married. It was the daughter and her husband who had found her, coming to visit.

The front door wasn't forced; the back door was locked. Mrs. Hopper was knifed and dead on the living-room floor, and the place had been ransacked. At the moment the daughter was having hysterics at a neighbor's house, but eventually they'd ask her what was missing.

"No phone book," said Grace. "Maybe they used another excuse this time. They didn't get much at the Freemans', and I don't suppose they'd have got much here. What we've heard about this Benoy, maybe just mean by nature, doing what comes naturally."

"Could be," agreed Higgins. "Could also be, careless about his prints as he seems to be, he's left some here too." They'd thought at first the Freemans might have been killed by someone who thought he still had the church collection money, but now the prints had been identified as this Benoy's, it looked like just the random thing, and this bore the same general appearance.

They called S.I.D. and imagined how the men would be cussing, a new one to work turning up at this end of shift. Higgins and Grace could go home, and hear what the lab had got tomorrow.

The wired prints of Benoy's sidekick came in from West Virginia; by then there was an A.P.B. out on Benoy. It would be nice to know what he was driving, but there wasn't a clue about that.

Alison was, she said, definitely better. The doctor had said it was just a question of time, and it didn't usually last beyond the third month. Cats twined under their feet at the dinner table, and Cedric paced up and down looking for handouts.

Mairí came to summon them to the ceremonial good nights, and for once Terry and Johnny looked and behaved like angels, too tired from a full day for anything else.

"The darlings," said Alison. "I was ready to murder

them yesterday, but a settled stomach makes a great difference. And by the way, I found out something very funny today," she added as they went back down the hall.

"*¿Qué ocurre?*"

"Well, I sent for this brochure," said Alison rather guiltily. She picked it up from her armchair and sat down, not offering to show it to him. "Houses. Bigger houses on, well, some land. If you're going to have a drink, I'll have some crème de menthe, *amado.*"

"I wasn't, but I'll get it." In the kitchen, he said to El Señor resignedly, "She's going to move us to a ranch now." El Señor uttered a raucous demand for rye, and Mendoza poured him some in a saucer. When he got back to the living room, the other three cats were all trying to settle in Alison's lap at once.

"You can't all fit now, and just wait a couple of months," she said, shooing Sheba and Nefertite off. "Thanks, *amado.* Well, it's very funny, you know I said maybe an acre, but come to find out, we've got nearly an acre here. It's forty-five thousand square feet, and I figured it out—we've got forty-two here. And we really need more—"

"I didn't know that," said Mendoza absently.

"Neither did I. Luis, you're not listening."

"I was wondering whether Carey had had a look at that vacant lot. But of course he did. *¡Diez millones de demonios desde el infierno!*" said Mendoza to his rye. "It's such a simple little mystery, and yet so vague. What the hell could have happened to the man?"

"Who? Now, I think, it's been some time since you brought any homework from the office," said Alison.

"You haven't been—mmh—in the exact mood to listen. But if you have any bright ideas about Edwin Fleming, I'd like to hear some." He sat down and told her about it, and she listened interestedly.

"Well, that's the funniest thing you've had in ages," she said when he'd finished with Galeano's account of today's interview. "You can think of explanations, and then you see it's impossible because of his being in the wheel-chair. And she couldn't have— And if I know all you hardheaded cynics, you turned every stone looking for a boyfriend, and there just isn't one."

"En ninguna parte," said Mendoza bitterly. "No-where."

"Well, all I can say is, I'm sorry for Detective Ga-leano," said Alison. "She sounds like a very prickly sort of girl. And speaking of sex, by the way, I've also been sitting up taking enough notice to think about some names—"

Mendoza uttered a groan. "I haven't dared ask about that."

'Well, I haven't decided anything yet."

Conway had wandered around all day Thursday on the Peralta thing, and got nowhere. He and Glasser were off on Friday, and Peralta fell to Landers, Grace and Higgins being busy on the new one, Palliser cleaning up Sandra Moseley and on the phone to Fresno, and Hackett in court: Roy Titus was being arraigned this morning. Wanda Larsen said she'd like some street experience, and if they came across any of Peralta's girl friends she might be help-ful, so Landers let her come along.

They had turned up some known acquaintances of Peralta, three men he'd been picked up with at various times, all users: Ford Robinson, Joe Ryan, Bob Wooley. That kind tended to drift, and none of them was still at the addresses they'd given on arrest. But Conway had talked to a fellow at one of those places who said Robinson had a pad over a disco on Vermont, The Aquarian. Landers looked up the address and he and Wanda started out in the new-to-him car. It was a nice little job, handled very sweetly; Phil had admired it.

The disco wasn't open, of course, but there was a rickety stair going up one side of the old stucco building, and they climbed it. At the top was a door painted a violent royal blue, and Landers knocked on it.

"You can't expect the free spirits to be up at this hour," said Wanda when he'd knocked five times.

"I can hear somebody in there." At the seventh knock the door was fumbled open.

"What the hell? What you want?"

"Mr. Robinson? Ford Robinson?"

"Yeah?"

"We'd like to ask you some questions about Rodrigo Peralta." Landers showed him the badge.

"Cops!" said Robinson disgustedly. "Cops, in the middle o' the night. A lady cop yet. What's with Roddy?" He yawned and scratched his chest. He was covered with so much hair that it was hard to tell what he looked like; he had a mane of wiry curly chestnut hair to his shoulders, he was only wearing shorts and his entire torso was covered with more, like his arms and naked legs.

Landers regarded him for a moment, considering the best approach to use. Wanda spoke up sweetly.

"We're looking for any friends of his who saw him last Monday night. To, you know, say where he was."

"Oh," said Robinson. "Like an alibi. I didn't see him Monday—more like last Saturday, maybe." He thought. "But I tell you who might of. Yeah, sure. The Kings."

"The Kings?" said Landers, not looking at Wanda.

"Yeah—Nita and Gerald. I run into them on Monday night, downstairs at the disco, they said they were going to see Roddy, see if he had—well, going to see him."

"I see," said Wanda, making businesslike notes. "What time was that?"

"Uh—seven, seven-fifteen like."

"Do you know where the Kings live?"

"Sure, they got a pad right back of here, on Thirty-first." He added the address. "They could prob'ly say Roddy wasn't wherever you thought he was. Damn cops coming—"

"Thank you very much," said Wanda prettily.

"Listen," said Landers on the sidewalk, "you're just supposed to be tagging along."

"Men," said Wanda. "You notice we got what we were after. I always believed the old adage that you catch more flies with honey than with vinegar."

Mendoza was sitting at his desk staring out at the Hollywood hills at three o'clock that Friday, the cards scattered on the desk behind him; he had spent an unproductive couple of hours brooding over Fleming. At least the rain had departed definitely; as usual in southern California after a rain, it had turned very cold, and it was brilliantly clear, the back mountains glistening with snow, the nearer hills sharply defined.

The office was quiet; everybody was out on something. The A.P.B. hadn't brought Benoy in yet. There ought to be a report from S.I.D. on the Hopper killing sometime today. A couple of autopsy reports were in; nothing much in them.

"*¡Ca!*" said Mendoza to himself. "*A su tiempo maduran las uvas.*" He got up and fished in his pocket for change for the coffee machine, and Sergeant Lake came in and shut the door behind him.

"We've got callers," he said. He was looking grim and rather pleased; he had one hand behind him.

"Anybody interesting?"

"Oh, I think so," said Lake. "I think you'll like her. A very respectable widow by the name of Mrs. Consuelo Gomez. She's got a mustache, seven sons, and a tender conscience."

"Meaning what, Jimmy?" Mendoza sat down again.

Sergeant Lake brought his hand from behind his back with something in it. He laid it on top of the cards on Mendoza's desk. Mendoza stared at it.

It was a large silver crucifix on a long silver chain. The center of the cross was studded with an opaque pale-green veined stone. It was, in fact, the crucifix which had been torn from Father Patrick Joseph O'Brien when the pretty boys attacked him.

Mendoza raised his eyes from it, and they had gone very cold. "Suppose you show the lady in."

"Oh, she's got one of them with her," said Lake. "Her youngest, Guido." He went out, and a minute later they came in. Mrs. Gomez was mountainous, in ancient and decent black silk, black hair piled in a knob on her head. But his eyes passed over her to the big boy behind her. Boy—he might be twenty, he was big but gangling: unused to his size as yet, awkward. Almost handsome, a poor attempt at a mustache, long waving black hair. And the very natty loud sports jacket, striped blue and green, a dark shirt, a wide tie.

She sat in the chair beside the desk and flooded Mendoza with emotion, religious and otherwise. "He is my youngest, my baby, I worry over him, I know he goes with these foolish young ones, and he does not come to church any more—I try to talk to him, I say—"

"Oh, for God's sake knock it off, Mama! You just wasting their time with your crazy ideas—" He gave Mendoza a calculatedly apologetic smile. "Listen, she's old country, know what I mean, you don't want to pay no notice, I didn't want to come here waste your—"

"You be still or I smack you again seven times! Oh, no, you don't want to come here, to police, and I am stupid and old, but I am yet your mother! I have to drag him here, he feels my hand hard—and maybe he should feel it more often since he thinks he is all grown to a man! Away from his so-clever modern friends, he comes with me, I see to that!" She was breathing asthmatically, and her little black eyes were bright. Queerly, for she didn't look anything like Teresa Sanchez y Mendoza, he was reminded of his grandmother.

"*That,*" she said, and pointed to the crucifix on the desk, "*that* is why! That, I find in his drawer! It will be—"

"For God's sake," he said, "for God's sake. I told you I found it. On the street."

"*That,* I know. It is the crucifix the priest at the church always was wearing. Father O'Brien. And he has been murdered, the other Father has told us, by these terrible wicked ones. I have seven sons," she cried emotionally, and all her chins wobbled magnificently, "and I thank the good God the six of them are decent Christian men, it is for my sins I have this wicked one—I tremble to think what he has done, if indeed it can be he has attacked a priest, but I know my duty to God and the law—I bring him to you!"

"For Christ's sake!" said the boy. "Of all the crap! I told you I found the damn thing, I thought it might be worth a couple bucks at a hock shop. That's all I know about it."

"Where'd you find it?" asked Mendoza.

"It was over on Fourth somewheres, just lying in the street."

"When?" asked Mendoza.

"Oh, Jesus' sake, couple o' days ago." He met Mendoza's cold eyes and suddenly backed away. "You aren't gonna believe the stupid old lady, I had anything to do— I found it!"

"I have known he is running with wicked ones, late at night, never would he tell me where he is, and sometimes drinking too much wine—I have implored him, take the good little job his uncle offers, earn the money—I do not know where he has money, his clothes—"

"Knock it *off!*" he said furiously. "For God's sake, all that crap about God and the law— That guy outside, he said Mendoza—I suppose you go for all that too, hah? I got shut of that a good long while back! Anything to all that, the hellfire, nobody in the world get out of it—I told you it was all in your silly Goddamn mind, you takin' a hand to me like I was still a kid—"

"I know my duty to God!"

"To hell with your stupid God! And these Goddamn cops, stupid damn pigs—" His eye fell on the gadget on Mendoza's desk, the life-sized pearl-handled revolver, and he laughed a little wildly. "Great big men, long as you got the guns around! You believe her, take me in and beat me up so I say anything—"

"Suppose we all calm down," said Mendoza. "Did you mention finding this to anyone, Mr. Gomez?"

"Goddamn all of you!" he said. And suddenly he made a grab for the gadget, snatched it up and turned it on his mother. "You Goddamned fool!" And he pressed the trigger.

Mendoza was on his feet. The barrel belched forth the

torch-like flame, and Guido Gomez dropped the thing and began to scream hoarsely. "Fires of hell—fires of hell— *fuegos del infierno*—I didn't mean to kill the priest, I didn't know he was a priest, I didn't mean—"

TEN

It took a while to calm him down. Sergeant Farrell shooed Wanda in three minutes later, when she and Landers came back, and she got Mrs. Gomez out and down to First Aid; Hackett came in and cowed Guido considerably by mere looks. Within ten minutes he was talking, sullen, reluctant, resentful, but talking.

They spelled it out for him that they knew there were three of them, and he came out with two names, Jay Folger, Bruce Hardwick. "We met up the semester I went to L.A.C.C. Goddamn it, you got me you're sure as hell goin' to get them—they been pullin' break-ins up in Hollywood for the bread, I wasn't in on that, I swear—" He gave them addresses: Emmett Terrace, Alta Loma Drive. "Jay, he drove me home one night, we saw that crazy old lady Miller lives at the end o' the block on her way home, he says have some fun with the old scarecrow, and we— No, we never got any loot off them, it was just for kicks. Goddamned old creeps, think they know it all, tell everybody else how to live— But that night—that night—I never knew it was a priest, till I saw his clothes."

Mendoza held up the crucifix. "How about this?"

Guido shivered and looked away. "I grabbed it—and then I was afraid, after, to hock it or anything. I shoulda put it in the trash, got rid of it, but I—and the Goddamned old woman—"

Mendoza sighed deeply and dropped it on his desk. "Take him away, Art," he said. "I do get so tired of the punks, the brainless louts."

Palliser was back then, and they all went up to Hollywood after Jay Folger and Bruce Hardwick. They didn't find either one. At the address on Emmett, a flustered middle-aged woman told them, "I don't know when either of them'll be home, Jay or his father—I'm just the housekeeper—Mr. Folger travels a lot for his company, and Jay, goodness knows where he is, he's got his own car."

At the Alta Loma address, Mrs. Hardwick stared at the badge in Mendoza's hand and said, "Police? What—what do you want with Bruce?" She was a fake redhead with a foolish face, a slack mouth, and she bleated like a sheep at them. "Bruce wouldn't do anything wrong, I see he has plenty of money of his own, he wouldn't—"

"God give me patience," said Mendoza.

Both of them were supposed to be attending L.A.C.C., but when the school was contacted the registrar said they'd both dropped out last semester. Eventually they would show up at their respective homes; the Robbery-Homicide men went up to the Wilcox Street precinct house and talked to Sergeant Barth, who said he'd have a squad car check at intervals, bring them in if they showed.

At least they knew who the pretty boys were; sooner or later they'd be in custody.

Mendoza went home to tell Alison what a successful gadget her Christmas present had proven to be.

* * *

With Guido coming apart, they'd have picked up Folger and Hardwick sometime; as it turned out, they were forestalled. Folger and Hardwick were out for some more lighthearted fun in the slums that night, and at nine-fifteen, having left Folger's sporty Jaguar parked on a side street, they had the misfortune to jump on Miss Maureen O'Connor. Miss O'Connor was tired, on her way home from work at a cafeteria uptown, and she was rather short-tempered by nature anyway.

"Come out at me like a pair of wild men," she told the uniformed men indignantly. "See me limping when I got off the bus, I s'pose, I twisted my ankle in the kitchen, and think they'd snatch my purse and I wouldn't do nothing—Hah! Fat chance I'd let 'em try! I just let 'em have it, and I bet they think twice, tackle a poor defenseless old woman again!"

"Defenseless?" said the Traffic man to his partner. "Well, it's not a very apt word for it. And listen, doesn't this look like the pair we had the word on at briefing? We better take 'em in to First Aid to start with." Miss O'Connor had felled Folger with one lusty blow of her heavy handbag, knocking him clean out on the sidewalk, and tripped Hardwick up and sat on him, yelling mightily for cops all the while. A nearby householder had obliged her by calling in.

So there they were neatly in jail on Saturday morning, and Mendoza and Hackett talked to them, not very long. They were saying various things about Miss O'Connor. "We had the word out on you already," Mendoza told them. "Your pal Guido told us where to find you."

"That Goddamn—I might've known, weak-bellied little spick!" Folger would have been the leader of the three, a dominating crude force like an aura about him. "Ever since we got that damn priest he's been ready to have kittens—" Hardwick just glowered.

"You do realize it'll be a charge of Murder One," said Mendoza. "It was just blind luck you only killed one of them. It really doesn't matter whether you're inclined to make statements or not." Folger growled and told them where they could go for statements. "So there's no point in wasting any more time on you two louts." Mendoza looked them up and down contemptuously. "Come on, Art." In the corridor they met Barth, who wanted to talk to the two louts about a few unsolved burglaries. "I wish you joy of them," said Mendoza. "I'm getting old, Barth. These punks without brains or bowels make me sick and tired."

Barth laughed and said, "You haven't changed in years, Luis. And I hear your wife's expecting again."

"More than that," said Mendoza. "Talking about moving to a ranch, I gather. And God knows, there are times I feel like buying a thousand acres in the middle of wilderness somewhere and building a fence around it and staying inside. What the hell are we doing at this thankless job?"

When he and Hackett got back to the office Landers was slouched at his desk rereading a report, and followed them into Mendoza's office. "This Peralta," he said. "No damned loss, but we have to do the routine. I've now got statements from three other people besides Ford Robinson that these Kings—Nita and Gerald—were at that disco on Monday night and said they were going to see Peralta. By inference, to see if he had any dream powder. I haven't turned up anything else. Walter Pepple, across the hall from Peralta, says it might have been two people running away.

And the Kings have taken off from their apartment. He had a part-time job at a service station, and the owner says he hasn't been in all week."

"So maybe we'd better put out an A.P.B.," said Hackett. "They sound likely for the job, Tom. At least we want to talk to them."

"I think so. I just put a query to D.M.V. about the car."

Hackett went out, heading for the sergeants' office, and met a diffident-looking couple in the hall. "Oh—Mr. and Mrs. Joiner."

"You asked us to come in, sir. Detective Grace said—"

"That's right," said Hackett. "Come in here." Carla Joiner was Myrtle Hopper's daughter. Hackett settled them down in front of his desk, and Grace and Higgins came over. The Joiners looked with faint awe at Higgins, that craggy man with cop all but emblazoned all over him, and were dumb before Hackett. Carla was small and pretty, her young husband round-faced and earnest.

"Just as we told you, Mrs. Joiner," said Grace easily, "all we want from you is some idea of what's missing from your mother's house."

"Well, there wasn't much there to steal," said Carla frankly. "Mother wasn't one for much jewelry or fancy things. But one thing we'd better tell you, her credit cards are gone. You people said we could go through the house yesterday, after you got finished looking around, and as soon as I looked I saw they were gone, she always kept them right in her wallet, and there was still a little change in it but the cards were gone."

"Which are they?"

"A BankAmericard and the gas company card. She

was careful about charging, but it was convenient, she always said."

Her husband broke in diffidently. "We'd like to know when we can, you know, fix up for the funeral."

"The coroner's office will let you know," said Grace.

"Is there any other family, Mrs. Joiner?" asked Hackett, the kind of random question to put witnesses at ease.

Her husband said, "I suppose we got to tell Isabel, Carla," and she just shrugged.

"I've got a sister, that's all."

"Nothing else is missing from the house that you noticed?" asked Grace.

"I don't think so, except her silver teapot. An old lady she used to work for gave it to her, and she treasured it a lot. I don't know what it'd be worth," she said miserably.

"Have you contacted the credit-card companies to let them know the cards are stolen?"

"Why, no—we never thought—we don't have any ourselves—"

"We can do that." Grace smiled at them, and had his mouth open to ask another question when Sergeant Farrell looked in the door.

"Traffic just picked up Benoy and Allesandro. It's a mess, sounds like—there was a high-speed pursuit down Victory and they rammed the squad—one Burbank man in serious condition, the squad wrecked, and wouldn't you know the two punks didn't get a scratch. Burbank's sending them in."

Hackett and Higgins got up in a hurry and went out, and the Joiners looked questioningly at Grace. "They're pretty hot suspects for your mother," Grace explained.

"We've been looking for them for another homicide, but we think it's possible they killed your mother too. One of them is definitely tied to the murder of those Freemans, more or less in the same neighborhood."

"Oh," said Carla. "I saw about that in the paper. It was awful. But I don't see how—I mean, Mother was always careful about locking doors and like that." They had both relaxed slightly, alone with Grace in the office. She looked at her husband. "It said in the paper you—the police—wanted to question some man about that murder, something about what it called an all points—"

"Bulletin," supplied Grace. "That's him. It's just turned him up."

"But," said Carla, "it said he's a white man. I forget all the description, how tall and so on, but he's white."

"Well?" said Grace.

Carla bent a solemn look on him. "Mr. Grace," she said, "Mother wasn't a fearful woman or one to borrow trouble as they say, but I've got to tell you, she'd never in this world have let a white man in her house after dark, the way it must've been. She'd never. Whatever they said as an excuse. A white man she didn't know. I just don't see how that could be, Mr. Grace."

Grace suppressed a laugh, looking at their earnest faces. "Well, it was just an idea," he said. "We'll see what they have to say for themselves."

What Benoy and Allesandro had to say was chiefly obscene. Hackett and Higgins questioned them at the jail, and it didn't matter much what they heard in regard to the Freeman homicide because Benoy at least was tied to that, but they asked some questions about Mrs. Hopper.

"I don't know what you're talkin' about." Benoy was

a big fat young man, gross and unshaven. "We never did nothing here. I don't know no Freemans or anybody named Hopper."

"Let's not go the long way round," said Higgins wearily. "We know you killed the Freemans, you left a nice set of prints on that phone book." Benoy began to swear, and his partner looked at him in sudden alarm.

"You said be careful about prints, Neal! You said to— I didn't leave any, did I?" he asked Higgins anxiously. He was a loose-limbed young fellow with straggly yellow hair. Hackett and Higgins didn't burst into laughter because they'd met a lot like him over the years.

"Not that I know of. Now let's talk about Mrs. Hopper, last Tuesday night." They were just guessing that that was when she'd been killed; the autopsy report should be in sometime today.

The two began arguing about where they'd been last Tuesday. They'd been living at an old hotel over in Glendale, but they didn't know the terrain out here and got confused about directions and distances. They agreed they'd spent last Tuesday night in a bar someplace, but couldn't say where.

"What the hell does it matter?" said Higgins to Hackett. "We've got them for the Freemans anyway. These days, a heavier charge means nothing."

That Saturday night was a busy one for the night watch, three heists and a market clerk shot dead in one of them. There were three witnesses to that, and Piggott, Schenke and Shogart were busy until the end of shift.

The witnesses came in on Sunday morning to look at mug-shots, and annoyed Galeano and Phil Landers. As witnesses sometimes were, they were confused by the very number of photographs to look at.

"I just couldn't say," said Akiko Tomito. "It all happened so fast—that looks like him, but so does this one, some—no, I guess this one here's more like, only his face was fatter—"

"Oh, dear me, I wouldn't like to say definitely," said Mrs. Marilyn Vail brightly. "If he'd had dark hair instead of light, he'd look a lot like this man—but then he didn't, so I guess it wasn't. On the other hand—"

"Nobody could say, just look at a picture," said Gus Severson with a growl. "Some pictures look like the people and some don't. I told you what he looked like. Couldn't say just from a picture."

Galeano suppressed any retort and thanked them for trying. "Description!" he said to Phil when they'd trooped out. "What the hell did they give the night watch? Six feet, five-ten, five-nine, medium, light, sandy, brown, sort of thin, kind of stocky, blue pants, black slacks, tan coat, white coat. I ask you."

Phil laughed. "The civilians aren't trained to notice things."

They'd be reduced to doing that the hard way, looking for men with the right pedigrees who fit the general description. And before they got down to it, they had a new homicide—a middle-aged man, Harry Schultz, a bookkeeper at a brokerage, stabbed to death as he walked up the drive to his own back door from the garage, just after dark. It was cold and misty, threatening to rain again, and nobody had been looking out windows or had doors open; even though it was a crowded neighborhood, houses on forty-foot lots, there were no witnesses and no leads. His wife said he might have had fifteen or twenty dollars on him.

"Round and round the mulberry bush," said Piggott, typing the initial report. "Just like ancient Rome, E. M. The weakened moral fiber, relaxation of standards, all the easy welfare, bread and circuses—*and* the pornography— and you get all the senseless violence, the killings done for peanuts, the killers given a slap on the wrist and let go to do it again. Makes you wonder where it'll all end, doesn't it?" He got no reply and looked up from the typewriter. Shogart had his feet propped up in Landers' desk chair and his head had fallen forward at an angle. He emitted a small snore. Shogart, up for retirement next year, had ceased a long time ago to get involved with the crime he was paid to look at.

Piggott sighed and went back to the report. "Sodom and Gomorrah," he muttered to himself. Talk about making bricks without straw—

On Monday morning, in a threatening gray mist, Palliser tried all the book's suggestions on Trina again, without much noticeable success. When it started to rain he came in, and Trina shook her wet self all over Roberta's clean kitchen floor. "You know, John," said Roberta, "I've had a look at that book too, and it says a few minutes every day, morning and afternoon. You can't expect to try once a week and get anywhere."

"Damn it, I'm busy all day and tired when I get home," said Palliser. "Even if I could get her to one of these classes—"

"Well, you're not accomplishing anything this way. I wonder how much it might cost to have a professional trainer do it?"

"Too much, if I know anything about prices these days. Yes, she's a very nice dog," said Palliser, sitting down and looking at the scratches on his shoes where Trina had been pretending to be a teething puppy again, "but why in hell did it have to be me who went out on that freeway accident? Just because I rescued Madge Borman's champion hound, so she has to give us one of his pups in a burst of gratitude—"

"Who I'm very glad to have around, she's a good watchdog. I'm home most of the day, you let me have a try at it."

"All I can do is wish you luck, Robin."

Hackett, Galeano and Higgins had gone out on the anonymous Schultz thing. Glasser and Conway were looking for possibles on the heist jobs, and Wanda was typing a report across the hall, when Jason Grace wandered into Mendoza's office on Monday just as Sergeant Lake put through a call.

"What's on your mind, Jase? Just a minute. Robbery-Homicide, Lieutenant Mendoza."

"Sergeant Richards up here in Santa Barbara," said a heavy male voice. "You've got an A.P.B. out on a Mr. and Mrs. King, sixty-three Ford sedan, plate AGN-740. We just picked them up."

"Thank you so much," said Mendoza. "We think they may be connected to a homicide here."

"Well, you'll have 'em on possession anyway," said Richards. "There was about a pound of marijuana in the car. Which is wrecked, by the way, they tried to run when the squad spotted them and King had a little load on and piled it up in a ditch. Do you want somebody to ferry 'em down there?"

"Well, we are a little busy," said Mendoza. "It'd be a nice gesture, thanks."

"Glad to oblige. I don't mind a little drive down the coast. Be with you sometime this afternoon," said Richards, and hung up.

Mendoza passed that on to Grace. He'd been sitting here practicing stacking the deck, and looked, as Grace told him, like an old-style riverboat cardsharp, hair over one eye where he'd run fingers through it, cigarette in mouth corner. "I've been brooding over Fleming, Jase. What have you got?"

"Just a little idea." Grace sat down and lit a cigarette. "This Mrs. Hopper. As George said, really not much M.O. about it, and Benoy and Allesandro denied it. The daughter told us her credit cards were gone, so I got on to the companies. Daughter also told me"—he grinned at Mendoza—"and don't say there's nothing to this race business, she'd never have come out with it to Art or you or George —that she's got a sister. Very unsatisfactory sister—they're all ashamed of her—lived around with this man and that, couple of illegitimate kids, on the welfare. Carla said Isabel had stolen things from Mother before, and it could be she'd helped herself to the cards, it mightn't have been the murderer."

"Interesante."

"I thought so. When I talked to the BankAmericard people—I didn't get any satisfaction on Saturday, of course—I just now heard that Mrs. Hopper had reported it herself, last Tuesday, and put a stop on any charges. Which looked possibly suggestive. I talked to Carla again and she told me her mother had put up with a lot from Isabel. Every time, Isabel all remorseful, never do it again, but she always did. And Mother wasn't playing any more."

"Are you heading where I think you are?"

"That's just where. Just for fun I looked in Records, and there's Isabel Hopper big as life. Soliciting, prostitution, possession, petty theft, and she's been tied up with a couple of mean characters. Maybe she still is, or could find one when she needed one."

"Probably," said Mendoza, his eyes on the cards. "And if Mother phoned her and said she knew who'd snitched her credit cards and this time she was going to prosecute—*Dios*, Jase, I have had it too, with these brainless brutes who hit first and think later! But that hangs together. Have you located her yet?"

"She's not where she was the last time she was picked up, but the welfare board will know where she is. I'm just waiting for somebody to come in to go with me, in case she's got one of the mean characters sharing quarters with her. I don't want to end up as a statistic in our files."

Mendoza laughed. "I won't volunteer. It's started to rain again. She's all yours, Jase."

Hackett had come in by the time Richards got there with the Kings. He shook hands around, said, "Glad to oblige. You've got quite a place here, haven't you?" He eyed Hackett interestedly, one big man to another. "If you don't want this pair, we do."

"Maybe you'd better hang around until we find out." Mendoza looked at the Kings, who were huddled together on the bench beside the switchboard. "Tom in, Art? He's the one decided we were interested." Hackett went to see, and came back with Landers. They shepherded the Kings down the hall to an interrogation room while Mendoza offered to show Richards around.

The Kings looked like birds of a feather. They were

in the early twenties, both with the long hair, both slightly scruffy and unkempt. Gerald King was short and sandy, with the red-rimmed eyes and persistent cough of the user; Nita was short and inclined to be too fat. They sat behind the little table and looked at the police fearfully, sullenly, defiantly.

"About Rodrigo Peralta," said Landers. "We've heard several people say you were going to see him that night, a week ago tonight. What about it, did you?"

They didn't look at each other, and neither said anything. "Come on, did you?" repeated Landers.

"No," said the girl. "No, we didn't see Roddy that night, not for a long time."

"Then why did you pack up and run away?"

"We wasn't running anywhere," said King. "We just went off on a trip."

"With Roddy's supply of marijuana?" said Hackett.

"It wasn't his, it was mine."

"Where'd you get it?" asked Landers.

"None of your damn business, pig."

It went on like that for quite a while, and Hackett and Landers were thinking it was a waste of time, until Landers happened to mention that one of their informants from the disco was Leona Petty. Nita turned on her husband and said, "I told you to lay off that bitch! You hanging around her again that night, sweet-talking her just because I danced a couple times with Rusty—"

"Couple times! You were with him half the afternoon," said King, "and I'll talk to who I damn please, and you can—"

"And you had to tell her we was going to see Roddy, ask for the grass, so naturally she spills it to the damn pigs and they—"

"Well, Jesus' sake, how'd I know what was going to happen when we got there, damn it? I never meant to kill anybody, did I? But—oh," said King. "Oh." He looked at Hackett and Landers. "Oh, hell."

"So why did you?" asked Landers.

"Him!" she said with an angry sob. "The big man! Roddy askin' too much bread, and he has to think, pull the knife and scare him, only Roddy tried to grab it—"

"Let's go book them in, Tom." In the corridor outside Hackett added, "I see just what George means. It's a wonder we retain any brains at all, associating with these—these so-called *homo sapiens*. I swear my five-year-old's got better sense!"

It stopped raining on Tuesday, but only momentarily, and on Wednesday the weather bureau made the front page: the most rain in one continual fall since 1877, but clearing promised for tomorrow and no more to come. Everybody made satiric remarks about that: wait and see.

Grace hadn't found Isabel Hopper yet; she hadn't been home since Monday, and the neighbor left to baby-sit the kids hadn't an idea where she was.

Higgins was off, and the rest of them wandering around looking for the possibles on the heist jobs. Hackett had come back briefly just as they had a call from Traffic to a new body. Swearing, he went out on that, passing Galeano on his way. It had somehow got to be two-thirty.

"Look," said Galeano, "we'll never get anywhere on this Schultz thing. Rich and I have been out on it, and there's nothing. Naturally S.I.D. didn't pick up anything at the scene, it was wet as hell. I vote we stick it in Pending now."

"Save time," murmured Mendoza, and Sergeant Lake looked in.

"You've got a visitor, Nick."

Galeano turned, and she came in uninvited, a little breathless, looking somehow different, more alive—Marta Fleming. She had thrown the hood back from her thick waving tawny hair, and under the coat she was wearing her waitress's uniform from the Globe Grill. She looked hopeful, uncertain, excited.

Mendoza stood up and said, "Mrs. Fleming."

"Marta—what is it?"

"I had to come at once," she said to Galeano. "At once when I read it—I could not believe it, but it is! It is! And, oh, if it should tell us—if he could tell us—what happened, where he is! That has been the nightmare, not to know. But I knew you must hear at once, I do not even change from my uniform, I must bring it—"

"Hey now, slow down," said Galeano. "Bring what?"

With shaking hands she set down her handbag on Mendoza's desk, a big worn brown leather bag, and unfastened the straps. She took out of it a fat envelope with two big green foreign stamps on it, the writing square, foreign-looking. She took the letter out, held it. "You do not read German? No—then I must tell you, explain what —how it is. I told you"—she was talking to Galeano—"how that day I remembered my letter to Elisa. How I came home to fetch it, to post it, and I was in such a hurry because of getting to the shops—so I fold up the letter and put it in the envelope and I rush off to post it."

"Yes. Take it easy, now. All right."

"Well! I told you also, we cannot afford to send letters by air, it is so expensive, even if it takes so long by sea—three weeks and more sometimes. But today—half an hour ago—I came home, and there is mail, and this letter by air mail from Elisa. She and Mama were so surprised—I—I had said nothing of all this, somehow I could not bring myself—I kept thinking, we should find out what happened and then I can tell them, he is dead. They could not understand it, but they knew it was important, so Elisa writes and sends it by air mail—"

"The letter? Why?" Galeano was slow on the uptake, watching her excited bright eyes.

"And this! *This!* It was the only writing paper in the apartment—I see just how it came about—my own tablet. Edwin used it, and left the sheet on top of my letter, and in such a hurry I must have gathered it all up together, put it in the envelope— But you see—you see! It is what I have said all the time, he meant to kill himself!" She thrust the whole sheaf of paper at Galeano.

Four, five sheets written closely in German. And the extra sheet—the same cheap stationery torn from a dime-store tablet—in another hand.

"*¡Media vuelta!*" said Mendoza, looking over his shoulder "*¡Ya está!* And how simple when you know. But what a damned queer—"

It was Edwin Fleming's suicide note, the scrawl of a man ill-educated and also probably half drunk—see what the lab experts said about that. *Dear Marta, I say good-bye and good luck. Youve been good to me and Im no use to you or anyboddy so I better get out of it Ill be glad to. Old Offerdol is goin to help me. You deserv better good girl I hope you find better life, Edwin.*

"I will be Goddamned!" said Galeano. "I will be—"

"Offerdahl!" said Mendoza, making it sound like a curse. "That drunken old bum—but he barely knew the man— *Porvida,* we'll hear what he has to say about this—"

"But I do not think so, immediately," said Marta. Suddenly she chuckled, a warm infectious chuckle that did funny things to Galeano. "Mr. Offerdahl—there was a terrible disturbance last night, he comes knocking at every door, shouting that God is bringing a new flood and we must run for our lives. And then he fell down in the hall, and I thought he was dead, but Mr. Del Sardo called an ambulance and the attendant said it was the D.T.'s. I do not know what—but he is in the hospital, and not dead, and please God he will tell us—"

Mendoza burst out laughing. "I only hope to God he isn't right—I want to hear about this!"

It was Thursday morning before Offerdahl was sufficiently dried out to talk to them coherently. Flat in the hospital bed, the first time they'd seen him sober and halfway sensible, he was weak and wan and remorseful. He blinked up at Mendoza, Galeano, Marta, and said, "Fleming. I was sorry for the poor fellow. Haven't—haven't you found him yet?"

And he'd asked them that before, but they hadn't realized how he meant it. "No, Mr. Offerdahl," said Mendoza. "We thought you could tell us where to look."

"Poor damned young fellow," said Offerdahl. "Felt sorry for him. Don't know what you think, but talk about sin, seemed a sin and a shame t' me he should have to go on living—maybe fifty years. Damn shame. Nice young wife, have to support him, take care of him. He said so. Said he wanted to die and be out of it. That day, I forget just when it was, I went down to see him—took a bottle along, cheer the poor fellow up. But he kept saying, better be dead—he wanted to be dead. Better for everybody. Like to go drown himself, he said. He asked me to help him and

I said I would. Reservoir in Griffith Park, he said, and his wife had some money hid away, he'd give it to me if I helped him. So I did. He had keys to the car, and I carried him out to it. Used to be strong as a bear," said Offerdahl, weakly flexing his muscle. "He left a note for his wife. Didn't she find it?"

"Eventually," said Mendoza. "Then what, Mr. Offerdahl?"

"I couldn't find the damn reservoir up there. Drove and drove, all round little winding roads, and it was raining like hell. Then we came to this place—that big building up on top of the hill." Griffith Park Observatory, the planetarium. "There wasn't anybody around, place all empty. He said, a cliff just as good, fall off it, bang. I drove right up there, helped him out—place where there's a wall round the building, big drop off the hill. He pulled himself up on the wall, and he said, just as good, and he fell over. The poor fellow. I 'greed with him—best for everybody. Sin and a shame—"

"And you drove the car back and put it in the garage, and put the keys back in the apartment," said Mendoza.

"Of course," said Offerdahl with dignity. "Wasn't my car. I'm an honest man."

When they went to look, they had to call the Fire Department with their ropes to get down there. But they found him after a while, deep in the underbrush there at the foot of the sheer drop from the wall around the observatory. It wasn't such a long drop at that to the first slope, maybe three hundred feet, and springy thick undergrowth below, but he was dead, and had been since that day. That was all wild growth in there, as through most of the park, and he might not have been found for years, until only bones were left.

"Of all the damned queer things!" said Galeano. "If that silly old bastard hadn't spent all Marta's hard-earned nest egg on whiskey— Yes, and didn't she and Mrs. Del Sardo tell us he'd never been so bad before, we might have wondered where he suddenly got the money—we'd have heard all about it as soon as it happened. If Marta hadn't grabbed up that note with her letter—"

"So simple when you know," said Mendoza. "Coming right back to human nature, Nick. And that girl—mmh—Alison said, prickly." He looked at Galeano with veiled interest.

"What the hell do you mean, prickly? With all she's had to put up with—"

When the autopsy report came in, Mendoza was sufficiently fascinated to carry it over to the other office to share it with somebody. Only Hackett was there. "Fate," said Mendoza. "By God, this is a funny one, Art—Fleming. He drowned, just the way he said he wanted to. The drop didn't kill him. He must have landed in a spot where the rain had collected in a pond, and the fall knocked him out and he drowned. *Allá va*. Of all the queer things, that is one for the books."

"Very funny," said Hackett inattentively.

"I must call Carey—he'll be interested. Little lesson for all of us, *tal vez*, about the automatic cynicism."

"Yes," said Hackett. "There's this new thing, Luis—you haven't heard about it yet—and it's damned funny too. This Hilda Gilbert. Divorcée, thirty-six, good job as a legal secretary, and alimony coming in. Found dead in bed this morning, strangled with a wire coat hanger. And she had quite a collection of good jewelry, a fur coat, new color

TV, and it's all there—no sign of burglary or forced entry. I got S.I.D. on it, but it looks like an offbeat one—"

Isabel Hopper and her latest heart interest came back from Las Vegas, and Grace and Conway picked them up for questioning. And Galeano finally got up nerve to call Marta and ask her to go to dinner with him on Sunday.

"It is not very proper, so soon after my husband— If it was a quiet small place, perhaps—"

"We'll find one. And I'll buy you some brandy, you seem to be a different girl with a drink or two."

"Now you are joking." But she laughed. "Very well, I will be ready at seven o'clock."

"Fate," said Alison absently. "Yes, it does make you wonder. That was one of the queerest you've had in quite a while." She was feeling fine, she said, and looked her usual self, red hair neat, in her favorite topaz robe. The cats were dispersed around her on the sectional, Cedric sound asleep at her feet. She was looking at the brochure from the real-estate company. "Luis, I've found a place I like. It sounds perfectly fascinating, let's go look at it on Sunday—*por favor, mi amador?*"

Mendoza opened his eyes and groaned. "I might have known."

"It's not new, but I think it'd be lots of fun to do up an old place. It's got six bedrooms and three fireplaces— I've decided it was a mistake not to have a fireplace here, there's something about an open hearth—and a wine cellar, and it's on four acres—such lovely room for Cedric—"

"How much and where?"

"Well, it's a hundred and sixty thousand, but when you think of the space—Hidden Hills," said Alison. "Well, really, Luis, you needn't yell at me, with the freeway it wouldn't be more than forty minutes—"

"Sin mujeres y sin vientos, tendramos menos tormentos," said Mendoza. "Females!" He leaned back in the armchair and thought about that divorcée. Hilda Gilbert. That could turn out to be an offbeat one indeed. . . .